I0739408

ELEVATOR MUSIC

ELEVATOR MUSIC

a novel by

KEVIN KLIX

This novel is the work of fiction. Any reference to real people, events, establishments, organizations or locales are intended only to give the fiction a sense of reality and authenticity and are used fictitiously. All other names, characters, and places and all dialogue and incidents portrayed in this book are the product of the author's imagination and are not to be construed as real.

FIRST EDITION

Designed by Kevin Klix

Library of Congress Cataloguing-in-Publication Date is available upon request.

ISBN: 978-0-9965410-4-6

To Madison Devine,
the girl who wanted to
. . . but then didn't.

ELEVATOR MUSIC

11:59 A.M.

. . . Beep! beep! beep!

12:00 P.M.

It starts like *this?* you're thinking. *Crap!*

This year, at 12:00 A.M., three months ago, on a "fun-loving" Friday, you decided that in kinda sorta exactly ninety days from that day, you were going to kill yourself, like gone, kaput, *zingo*, big brotha.

It's exactly eighty-nine days later and you're in the beautiful, lovely Sunshine State, the weather showing a perfect seventy-six degree day, and in twenty-four hours your self-execution will be commencing, surely.

And it's not like you're this typical depressive that the world blabs about on a daily basis. You're just, you don't know, kind of over it, you guess.

Someone is calling you right now while you're in your apartment, while you're packing the rest of your stuff in your crumby ole backpack—matches, shirts, water, fireworks, extra change of underwear, et cetera, et cetera. And, briefly, while you read a disconnection notice from a cellphone company

(AT&T? Metro? Sprint?), you're thinking, It doesn't matter, now.

You put on your backpack, still hearing the cellphone ring. You look down, reach into your pocket, and pull out your phone, seeing the screen. Oh, gosh. Rob's calling. You roll your eyes and sigh to yourself, "Oh Jesus, take the wheel . . . this friggin' kid." You click accept, placing the phone to your ear.

"Uh . . . sup, Rob?"

"Bro! We on for today?"

What is he talking about? you think. *On* for today? You didn't make any plans, did you?

"No, getting evicted . . ." you say.

"*Evicted,* huh?" he asks.

You sigh. "You don't pay, you don't live, Rob."

He pauses, and then, "Could you, like, meet me at Starbucks, bro?"

"Guess so . . ." You really don't want to.

Then he goes, "And could you—"

But you interrupt him. "Hang on, *hold* up . . ." Putting the phone away from your ear, you hear something. "*Hello?*" you say to the noise. "What's up?"

A deep, tough voice behind your apartment's door says, "Open up. Rise 'n' shine, lil' man."

You put the phone back to your ear, saying to Rob, "I gotta go. Meet you in fifteen." You hang up.

You hear thick, heavy knocking. "Open! Up! NOW!"

"Coming!" you say. "Hold up!" You go up to the door, knowing this was coming, and then you open the door and you wince just a lil' bit.

"Hey, you," your old landlord says. "Where's my money?"

"Stopped paying," you answer, smirking, though you don't really know why you are.

"Guess who doesn't have a place to stay . . ." He grabs your shirt and pulls you out the door, hurling you across the hallway outside your old apartment. And you, *bang!* hit against the wall, hard, smacking the shit out of your noggin'. "*Crap!*" you say. Loud as all hell. "You can't just *do* that!"

"Just did," your landlord says, grinning that devilishly conniving grin, the bastard. He slams the door shut while inside your old apartment's doorway, probably just about to throw all your belongings out, whatever.

"Jesus, take the wheel," you seem to say again to yourself. "Twenty-four hours left. Just. Make it. Through. The day. *Crap!*" You keep looking at your wristwatch, it being this weird, magical thingy that is pretty much your fate, your life, your death, your everything, and you seem to sigh to yourself, yet again, like you always do, because life just, you know, sucks big massive donkey butt, or whatever. . . .

12:08 P.M.

Inside the elevator leading down to the bullshit you're about to face is, uh, the elevator guy that you always see every morning before you walk off to work. And this elevator guy tips his little monkey hat the same way he always does for you and this makes you pretty envious of him, even though he is in fact just doing his job and he really doesn't care enough to greet you in your little—

"Having a good day, mister?" he asks, cutting off your little thoughts about your meaningless life, you think.

"Yeah," you say. "Just piss off and do your job."

"Okay, boss," he says, squinting, hating you entirely to some extent. Then he asks you, nicely and very professional-like, "What floor, boss?"

"Bottom."

"Okay, boss."

A random, weird, embarrassed wince happens to you involuntarily. The elevator guy presses the button. You and him go! Down that is . . . Both silent the entire time (go figure) since you're an asshole/dickhead who maybe has maybe no interest in the elevator guy's maybe thoughts. The doors open. Dark, light, bright. Screw life.

12:12 P.M.

You go to your parking garage and see your black Honda Civic, old and withered and super '90s-looking, you think, and then you click the alarm button on your keys to make a bunch of noise because you think, Who gives a crap, right? It echoes so loud that the tollbooth-type security guard thingamajigger, black, mid-forties, tallish, not American, presses his ears with his palms and closes his eyes and yells, "What the *hell*, kid! SLOW DOWN!" and you just laugh, finally coming up and getting into your car. Key in ignition, drive on off. Today's a good day, you kinda sorta think. Rock on. Whatever. Pull out. Drive, drive, drive. Turn here, cut through there . . . Duh! Park at Starbucks.

12:18 P.M.

"You're late," Rob says as you enter Starbucks.

"So sue me then," you say back, putting your backpack on the table he's ever so lazily lounging at, the asshole.

"I'm just kidding, yo. Don't have a hissy-fit."

"Whatever."

You turn, start to walk up to this lovely blonde Barista—so damn fine.

Rob stops you. "Hey!"

You turn your head around. "*What*, goddamnit."

"Sit."

You spin your whole body back around, doing as he says, whatever.

"Always chasin' tail, my niggie," Rob mocks you with a F-ed-up, crooked smile.

"So . . . ?" you mutter.

"How come you haven't been returnin' my phone calls?"

"Busy."

"With what?"

"Don't wanna talk about it."

He squints.

You squint, too, but you get up.

"Get me a mocha frappe," Rob says.

You're like, "Yeah, yeah, yeah, whatever."

12:22 P.M.

You walk up to the line, backpackless, hands in your pockets, and it's not crowded at all. And you hear this old lady in front of you, her turn at the register, and she's talking with a friend about how she thinks the young people of today, also known as the "newly adults," as she lamely puts, are all so far up their asses that it's not even funny.

As you hear this, you snicker, because you totally think it's completely true.

"What?" the old lady asks you. "It's *true!*" She probably thinks you don't agree.

"Whatever, bro," you say to her.

She squints.

Finally she gets done ordering her one-thousand plus calorie drink, and walks on off. . . . Your turn now. You see the blondie.

"What can I get you started with?" she asks you.

"Mocha Frappe and a Trenda Ice Coffee."

"Outta Mocha, sorry sir."

"Oh . . ."

You pause.

"Caramel, sir?"

"Yup."

She rings you up.

"Cream, sugar," you inform her cute self.

"What?" She squints.

"Lady, hey. Can I ask you somethin'?"

"Sure, but make it kind of quick." Her voice is trying to be composed but sweet with you.

You clear your throat—"Eh-*hem*"—and then ask her, "Would you make out with me?"

This startles her. "I have a boyfriend," she, in her nicest way possible, says.

You grin. "Is that *so?*"

"Yeah . . . ?"

"What's his name?" you ask, thinking this bitch doesn't have shit of a boyfriend, much less an actual *name* for him.

"Uh . . ." she starts, and you think it's kind of sad.

So you say, "Knew it, yo."

"—Greg!" she finally answers. "His name is *Greg*."

You just laugh at her lying self, the bitch.

"Sir, is that all you *need?*" she basically spits out.

"Yeah, whatever, yo."

Her being monotone: "Okay . . . ?"

"Sure, sure, sure," you say.

Bitches . . . bitches . . . bitches, your brain tells you.

She says your total and you don't hear it, you just swipe your debit card with a whooping whatever-whatever on it. You vaguely look at your watch after. Wait . . . wait, *wait!*

12:32 P.M.

Feels like an hour that you've been in line, but it's pretty typical because of how busy, how packed, this Starbucks in particular is.

"S'today slow?" you ask someone, anyone, anyway.

The Starbucks manager comes up and brings you your two coffees, saying to you, "Sorry, here's a coupon, sorry sir, I apologize."

Wow.

So you take it, ruthlessly, angrily pocketing it, knowing that you probably won't use it considering you only drink this shit in the mornings and you're deader than dead meat soon, or in a couple of hours.

But you say, with your fake smirk, "Thanks, or whatever . . ." You walk on off. Oh hey, Rob. *Sike!*

12:33 P.M.

He's like, "Took long enough, bro."

"Here's your bullshit," you retort, putting down his drink but sipping on yours.

"Jay kay, niggie." He sip sip sips on his straw.

Silence hits.

"Bro . . ." you say, killin' it, "today's not good."

"Why's that?" Rob asks, the tips of his fingers around this F-ing heart attack in a plastic cup, green circle of a happy sea-monster between them.

"Let me ask you something," you say.

"Shoot, kid."

"What do you think of suicide?"

Rob goes silent.

"Just asking, jeez . . ." you say. Slurp, slurp. *Ahhh.*

"I think it's the easy way out," Rob comments.

"Yeah, but what if it's the only way?"

"How could it be?"

"Well—for example, um, what if you just didn't like how life ran? Like how people treat each other and whatever."

He squints.

"Huh?" you sigh, not wanting that reaction.

He goes, "I guess that's very bleak—but look, let me be honest. You thinkin' 'bout doin' it?"

"I've decided that at twelve o'clock **P.M.** I'm going to kill myself." You run your thumb over your neck, *keek!*

"But why, yo?" He takes a sip.

" 'Cause . . . I'm, uh . . . over it all."

"I should probably stop ya, kid. I'd be a pretty screwed-up friend if I didn't."

"You won't be able to."

"So why at twelve **P.M.**?"

"Well . . ." You smile. "I have a few things up in the ole brain."

Rob smiles, harder. "I see . . . Like?"

"Wanna do everything that I'd never do, ever."

"Bro, how about this: What if I show you a good time, then when the time comes to, uh"—he scratches his head—"kill yourself, you can make the decision."

You laugh. "We'll see, yo." You start to get up. "We'll definitely seeeee," you sigh. . . .

And Rob's like, "Just outta curiosity, what do you have planned?"

"Play by ear—I don't know. Know that girl I like?"

"Shelby?"

"Yeah. Her."

"Yeah . . . ?"

"I wanna just make out with her."

"Where does she live?"

"Don't know."

"Could ask around."

Grabbing your backpack, you go, "Get up, yo. Don't have time."

"Right, right," Rob says. "LETS PARTY!"

How F"ing cliché, you think.

Leave. Walk. Keys. Car. Drive. Time:

12:51 P.M.

Rob, sitting down in your car, is laughing about this one college bitch named Tessa, who's a brunette, has huge tits, fat ass, attitude to hell, who he "messed around with" about a week or so ago, and he feels his phone vibrate in his pants and you both hear its ringtone, Drake's "Started From The Bottom." Rob probably knows who's calling, the college bitch, also being Shelby's friend, whatever. No shit? And you just sit there, jealous, joy-riding south along Dixie Highway at seventy miles-per-hour and about to cut a deadly sharp left turn onto Royal but then miss it completely and then you hear Rob, his voice all joker-ish and flirty, talking into the phone, the convo you hear only from his end, his voice going on, like, "Yo, girlie. . . . What up? . . . Chillin', you? . . . Hey, listen. Know that girl Shelby? . . . Yeah, that one. . . . Yeah, yeah. . . . Yeah. Know where she stay? . . . No, not tryna *fuh!* God! . . . Nah, tryna help a friend out . . . She is? *Oh!* Oh, okay. . . . Where do she live? . . . Okay, okay. . . . Cool. . . . Do NOT let her know, yo. . . . Okay, bye, love ya . . ." and you feel this overwhelming hatred at the fact that he ended the convo with "I love you" because you both know that it's the furthest thing from being true, and though Rob acts normal about it, completely normal, he says to you, "Found her. Turn down Flamingo then cut a right. Her house is a purple one or something. Number 1440, whatever, yada-yada." This, again, makes you utterly jealous because you think you're too much like a goddamn pussy. Then you think, too, that you probably won't go through with this, the, um, whole confession thingama-jig. . . . Arrived!

1:05 P.M.

You're outside your crush's house, in your car, creepin' up, your friend Rob next to you, and you notice your crush's house is absolutely beautiful, with its great gardening, its tree out front with a tire swing, its utter girlie-ness you love so damn much, and then you step on the brake finally and, nervous as all hell, you say to Rob, "I'm nervous as all hell," and he goes, "Just do it.

Chicks are easy," and then you ask, "What do I say?" and then, laughing, he goes, "Anything, bro! Just say something honest. Like you wanna fuh, fuh, *fuh*" and you just shake your head at how stupid this nig is, the lame-O.

1:08 P.M.

Looking at your watch, you feel this sensation of heat flowing up your chest and to your face, but this shouldn't be happening since you think you have nothing to lose, but still having this F-ing *happen,* you beezy, you're taking strides up your crush's lawn, the grass perfectly cut, the sprinklers on, the red brick walls circling around the house, the purple car parked, the blue F-ing door, and then, walking closer . . . closer, closer . . . you see a lawn gnome, a stair step, then another, then another, and you keep walking up, seeing a cement porch, a blue door in your face, a small, over-the-top window looking into a living room, but you hesitate, looking back around at your friend Rob in your car as he yells, at the top of his lungs, "GET IT, SON!" and though this is the scariest thing you've ever encountered, you laugh, turning back around, putting your hand up and knocking your knuckles on the blue door, vaguely hoping nobody answers but at the same time wanting them to. Then you hear a sweet voice, after about a couple of seconds, say, "Coming!" and the very thought of the seconds reminds and runs over your head so much so that you look at your wristwatch and see

1:10 P.M.

"Hello?" the same sweet, gentle voice says behind the door, a voice you have heard before in City Place once or twice vaguely in the past or some kind of something.

You look up and, a quick gasp and heart-sink, you see the most beautiful thing ever in the blue door's window, the eyes a perfectly brown color but having a slight hazel tone to it, the cheeks up, smiling, the teeth so white that it makes you jealous and you think how in the world this chick can make them that bright-white. Was it Crest? Bleach? Arm & hammer? You don't know. But that shouldn't run over your head, so you come back to "the now," as your friend Rob puts it, and you say to the voice, "Uh, hi," waving your hand like a goof-ball slash jackass.

The door opens. "No way!" your crush, Shelby sweetie-pie-awesomeness, says. "That *you?* Holy, wow!"

"Hey." You scratch your head, so nervous that you almost feel psychosis running over your entire being, your entire short little life. "Um . . . you know me?"

She says yeah and that you're your name, whatever, which is ______.

"Huh?" you ask, not getting it.

She goes on like, "Yeah, I work near your job on Clematis. Pizza Luna, right?"

Depressive as hell, you say, "Quit the other day."

"What!" She leans back, baffled. "Wow. I work at the hookah bar next door. Always be seein' you."

"Always see you too."

"Yeah, why don't you—*Wait!* Why are you even *here?* If you don't mind my asking."

You go silent, the brick walls start to bend, her voice goes all echoey, your eyes start to close, and then, quickly, you shake yourself, trying to come back to "the now," but afterward you hold your head, only slightly embarrassed and you realize your anxiety is raising.

"You okay?" Shelby asks you.

"Yeah, I'm fine. Just have a few monkeys on my back, is all."

"A few *monkeys* on your back?!" She squints. "Can I help with that?"

"Yes, actually."

She keeps on listening.

"Well, uh . . . I came here because . . . uh, because I've been . . . uh . . ." You look down at the ground, scratching your head.

"What?" she says, her voice really sweet and concerned. "What's wrong, hun?"

Still looking at the ground, you go on like, "I'm usually not too forward, but . . . um, I've had a crush on you for months now, probably even a whole year. I see you walking down

Clematis with your uniform on and working and acting so nice to people from afar, and I just can't help but smile. For the longest time—Actually, still being the, um, case, I think you're the most beautiful thing I've ever seen. I've been very, very chicken to say this all to you, but today is a very special day for me, and I thought that I should finally say this to you because . . ." You stop. You feel an index finger pick your chin up and you are looking directly at the face of your crush.

She smiles. "That's better. Eye contact," she tells you. "Please continue, love."

This move is so adorable that you just melt inside with lame-ass butterflies, that it almost leaves you speechless, but you keep going on and on, like, "I love the way your voice sounds, I love the way you walk, I love the way you talk, the way you carry yourself, the way you smile, the way you look so, uh, confident, the way you look. . . . I really love everything about you, but I don't even know you, and that's the thing: For the longest time I've just thought of myself as some guy that would be trying to hit on you if I were to approach you, but it wouldn't be like that. I would treat you very nice and special, like a princess, as corny as that sounds." You laugh. "But, uh, yeah, and also I just want you to be happy with me, and forever I've just wanted to kiss you, hold you, touch you, hug you, take you out, date you, dine with you, take you to the movies—"

Your crush interrupts. "Okay, okay!" She seems excited as all hell! "Jesus! I love this! Okay, yeah! Okay. I feel the same way too! I always stare at you when I walk passed my job's entrance; even during lunch when I order from you sometimes."

"Oh yeah?" you say, smiling with satisfaction. "Wowie."

"I know, love. But here, um . . ." She quickly as heck leans into you, kiss kiss.

Your face feels hot and you feel your stomach tickle.

"I approve," she says.

Your crush totally suffices, you guess. Wow. She kissed you. Vaguely you think she's either too easy or actually in love with you to some extent. Maybe it's the vegetables she possible eats. Maybe she's just adventurous. It's probably a little of everything. You look at your watch.

1:14 P.M.

"Hey," you say to her after. "Do you wanna spend the day with me? I know this is a bit forward, but I might as well be a bit forward, 'cause I'm already being, um, forward." That was a stupid way of wording your shit, you think, but whatever.

"Oh yes, love." She grins, steps forward, loops her arm into yours.

You hear Rob shouting, "My niggie, my niggie!"

This makes you utterly embarrassed. "That's my friend, though," you say to Shelby, eyes rolling, head shaking. Stop. "I hope you don't mind."

She grips you tighter. "The more, the merrier."

You both walk.

You are holding open your car's passenger-side door and your lovely crush, Shelby, sits on in, snug, and you think about her being naked for a sec, but then you snap out of it and don't possibly think she will sleep with you today, considering you literally just met her, and then the realization hits you that you just showed up at her house and she's down to hang with you for the whole damn day. . . . Awesome. Mission accomplished?

1:17 P.M.

You sit in your car, strap seatbelt on, hold the wheel, turn on music, whatever.

"You guys smoke?" Shelby asks.

"I like her already," Rob says.

You're like, "I don't smoke, but Rob here does."

"Oh goodie!" Shelby says. "Here." She goes into her pocket and pulls out a bowl and a baggie.

You turn down the music, low.

After a moment, while Shelby is packing a bowl, she hums the song "Wouldn't It Be Nice" by The Beach Boys, and this makes Rob go on singing about if we were older, and then we wouldn't havta wait so longgggg, and Shelby giggles at this.

You sigh, thinkin' Rob is gonna bag her before you do, the F-ing bastard.

"You're not gonna smoke?" Shelby asks you. "Hm?"

You shake your head no.

"Pity." She lights the bowl with a lighter that came from out of nowhere.

After, though, coughing, she hands the lit bowl to Rob and he sucks in the smoke, deep, then leans between your seat and Shelby's after and blows smoke out and at your face, saying, "Straight-edge kid."

This lil' bit of disrespect, that to normal people in your town would think isn't a big deal, is what makes you want to kill yourself, off yourself, *gone*. Kaput. Zingo!

"Hey, chill," Shelby says.

"Sorry," Rob apologizes, sitting back down.

Skipping a beat, you ask them both, "Where to?"

"Smoke with me," Shelby demands.

"No." Then you think about how retarded it would be to have never . . . Then you say aloud, "Smoked."

Shelby squints, saying, "What?" not hearing your inner thoughts because she's not an F-ing psychic.

"Nevermind. Lets do it," you say, holding your head now.

Rob leans over and hands you the bowl, it still being lit and crackily, and then you're holding it front of yourself, eying down at it, the half-green, half-cashed cush looking and smelling like pure skunk, and then you raise it to your lips and draw in, hard.

For a second you think that Shelby is a straight up G to have shit that's as dank as this. But then you feel like you took in too much smoke so you, *ah ah ah,* start freaking out and coughing. Probably ate the damn smoke. And you lean over, choking and coughing, and Shelby taps your back and goes on, like,

"Breathe, it's okay, *breathe!*" and then you finally stop, but drool is slipping between the cracks of your teeth and over your lips, over your chin, and you feel hella embarrassed/scared.

"Shit, son," Rob says to you, then asks, "You iight?"

You nod. "I'm fine."

"You smoked it wrong," Shelby informs you, the lil' bitch.

"My first time," you cough out.

Rob and Shelby, at the same time, go, "WHAT?!"

You laugh, coughing almost, and say, "Yeah."

"Wow," Shelby says. "Just . . . wow."

"Where we goin'?" Rob asks.

"Don't know," you say.

1:28 P.M.

You're driving back down Dixie at about one-hundred miles-per-hour and Shelby is screaming "yeah!" the whole time, and Rob is completely indifferent.

He goes, "Laaaaaaaame."

You go, "Piss off!"

She goes, "YEAH! WOO-HOO!"

And you realize how high you are, you *all* are. The roads seem like they are like waves, but whatevs, you don't care. Life is kind of good right now.

You put on some Mac Dre through your iPod connected by the auxiliary cord.

"I love this song!" Shelby says, all hyped. The song is called "Cadillac Cars."

"WHAT!" you say, so impressed and surprised that you smile wide. "How in the world do you know this?!"

She sings along, "Three-fifty-one—eh-*hem!*—I think make the old school swifter?"

And you go singing about rapping in the trunk, slapping on the trunk.

Fat four-fours in your guys' laps for the funk.

And talking to a no-good beezy on the phone but you can't hear her.

And turning down the "humps" so, um, you can hear clearer?

And hearing maybe sirens get nearer.

And Shelby ends it with the red, blue lights in your rearview mirror, or something.

And, ironically, you look in your rearview and see red and blue lights flashing. "Oh shit!" you say.

Shelby turns down the music. "Keep cool," she says. "I'll handle this. Pull over."

You do. Then—

1:33 P.M.

Wow. You are pulled over. Shelby asks you if you have your I.D. or whatever.

"Yeah," you say.

She sighs. "Good. Thank God."

After a bit, you see the cop walking toward you in your rearview.

He comes up to your window, tapping his knuckle on it, blurting, "Hey!"

You roll down your window. "Yes, sir?"

"You have any idea how fast you were going, son?"

Shelby goes, "I'm sorry officer, is there any way to repay you?" She bats her eyes. Maybe even a wink.

He grins, going, "May*be*, ma'am," then, to you, "License and registration." Does he know her?

You go into your glove compartment and pull out the shit. You hand it over.

The cop inspects it. "Good. Good." He hands it back. "I gotta still give you a ticket for going sixty-five miles over the speed limit." He pulls out a slip. "Policy, you understand."

Bat, bat, Shelby immediately lifts her shirt up, flashing her big, big, tan double-D tits, the nips small and pink and perfect. Oh your god!

You're looking at her, wide-eyed, and then you look at the cop, still wide-eyed.

He goes, "On second thought . . . nevermind." He puts the slip back into his pocket. "Those are nice. Have a good one, folks."

Shelby smiles, saying, "Thanks!"

The cop walks away.

You quickly roll up your window, still wide-eyed as heck, not believing this bull.

"Wish *I* could do that," Rob says.

"A gift," Shelby says.

"Those things are nice."

"One time deal." Trying to probably gain validation, Shelby turns to you, quick, asking, "But um . . . d'you like 'em, hun?"

Looking down at your watch, ignoring her, you go, "Wowie, yo—would you look at the time!?"

1:55 P.M.

"D'you like 'em, hun?" Shelby asks you again. "Don't pretend like you don't hear me."

You look up. "What do *you* think?"

She bats her eyes. "I'm wild, aren't I, love?"

"No comment." You smile, starting up your car.

"I'll take it," she laughs.

For a while now, you all three, you, her and Rob, the bad-ish bad-bads ever to be badasses in the land of badass, just listen to various kinds of music, driving normal, and you finally get down to the lovely world of downtown, City Place, the coolest of the coolios, *bro!*

2:12 P.M.

"Park there!" Shelby says. "Valet!"

You cut into the spot.

"I'll pay!"

"Cool," you say.

You unlatch your seatbelt.

Shelby and Rob both get out; you too.

Outside is bright as all the cares of the world, so you go back into your car and open up the middle console and bring out and put on some red Raybans (neato!), but also you look at your backseat and unzip your backpack and pull out some firecrackers and some matches and pocket them.

You close your door and walk around your car, noticing Shelby saying to the valet boy, all being sarcastic, "MmmMmm, fancy parrr*king!*"

He just shakes his head, snickering, giving her a number card.

You toss your keys over to him, he catches.

"So," Shelby says to you as you step onto the sidewalk, you hearing your car starting up. "Where to, love?"

Rob is looking off into the large clusters of crowds in the courtyard.

"Where to?" Shelby repeats, a bit on the irritated side.

"Well, uh, I've been wanting to do something for a while now," you answer.

"Yeah? And what's that?" Her voice is all of a sudden sweet.

"Dance on the courtyard's stage."

"What! No way! I've wanted to do that too!"

"Yeah, but I wanna do it in front of everyone."

"Yeah, yeah! Lets do it!"

You guys knock yourself out," Rob says. "I'm gonna holler as some honeys and laugh at you guys from afar."

"Whatever!" Shelby playfully scolds, whatever. Then she loops her arm into yours.

Rob walks off. You look at the hexagon-tiled ground and see a melted ice cream cone that had been dropped by probably some kindergardener earlier in the day or some shit.

Shelby walks you along.

There's a million, zillion shopping centers and a million, zillion, trillion people, but this doesn't faze you because everything feels like . . .

"Feels like I'm free to do anything I want," you say aloud, not thinking.

Shelby goes, "That was random."

You see a ballon stand and kids getting balloons and parents buying them. You see Sunglass Hut, Zephora, Starbucks, Barnes & Noble, et cetera, and hella hot chicks buying clothes at whatever the hell outlets they shop at—you don't know the names of them.

It's loud.

"What music are they playing?" you ask Shelby.

She looks up at you, arm still looping yours. "Don't know, love. Sounds tribal."

"I'm SUPER nervous."

"Why?"

"Never do things like this."

"It's just for fun. You're supposed to make yourself look a like tard."

"Yeah, yeah, whatever."

"Come on!" She pulls you along, your head flings back with the motion, and she's running, running toward the stage.

Wow. You see the staircase leading up to the stages and all of a sudden you picture yourself being laughed at by hundreds of people, all being men, women, and even children.

"Come on, love! Come!" Shelby is saying to you. You're pulled up the stairs. You look down at your—

2:22 P.M.

The stage is massive from this view, the view from being on it, no shit. The crowds seem endless, their heads are like little mops on sticks dancing up and down, you think.

Your heart is racing so fast, bump bump *bump!*

There's a record player on a stand, there's a microphone next to its speakers.

Shelby walks you toward them.

You look down at the record and it's Béla Fleck and the Flecktones, and you think that this isn't tribal at all, none whatsoever.

Shelby lets you go but leans down next the record player and sifts through a bunch of music.

"Here's one," she says.

She lifts up a record, it's Duran Duran.

"Hungry Like The Wolf!" she says.

"Wowie," you say.

She pulls out the record, slowly, carefully, and then stands up and lifts the needle on the record player, stopping the music.

The crowd completely halts. Ah, man, they all seem to say. Eyes are staring at you and Shelby.

While you're shitting bricks over it, this doesn't seem to faze her, not one teeny tiny bit; all she does is simply take off the Fleck and put in the Duran. She puts the needle to the right spot. "Hungry Like The Wolf" plays.

Everyone is looking at you and her, smirking.

"Oh shit," you say.

"Come on!" Shelby says, grabbing your hands.

She swings side to side, her hips gyrating and she crouches down and then goes back up. You're just kinda holding her hands and moving your shoulders slightly, awkwardly, all embarrassed.

"Come on!" Shelby repeats. She lets go of your hands and puts her arms up in the air and spins around and bumps her bum bum into you.

You hold her hips.

"WOO!" the crowd yells. "YEAH!"

You smile.

"Woo! Woo! Yeah! Woo!" the crowd keeps chanting, clapping to the music, *clap clap clap.*

You start moving Shelby around, spinning her, tango tango, circling your shoulders and moving back and forth. Wow, this feels awesome to you.

Shelby stops.

"Hey. Lets do something *crazy,*" she says to you.

She walks over to the microphone.

She announces to everyone, "Hey, everyone! This guy right here has had a crush on me for over a year now! Should he kiss me in front of all of you?!"

Everyone cheers. The stage feels wobbly and vibrating.

"Good!"

Shelby turns to you, steps forward, puckers up. . . . This is what scares you most—

You step forward, the crowd yelling and cheering at the top of their lungs, no music playing. "Kiss *her* . . . Kiss *her* . . . Kiss her!"

You're so hella timid that you close your eyes.

The crowd sings some "Sha-la-la"s, and "my, oh my"s.

This makes you smile, you feel warm. Disney is awesome, you kinda think. Unda da SEA!

More "sha-la-la"s, and "my, oh my"s happen.

You lean in, kiss kiss, hard, longer than you should, but Shelby doesn't mind, not one little bit.

Stopping this, she holds onto you, your hand supporting her lower back, and she waves at everyone.

You reach into your pocket, pull out the matches and firecrackers. . . . This should be fun.

Shelby looks at you and says, "Oh shit." She smiles. "Do it do it do it!"

You light a couple firecrackers and toss it into the crowd. They shout and yell and *scream!*

Pow pow pow! the firecrackers go.

While everyone is gasping and holding their heads and taking cover and running and reeking F-in' havoc, you watch check . . .

2:32 P.M.

You look up then back down for a sec, back at watch. . . .

2:33 P.M.

Shit. Time feels like it's flying; it just changed as soon as you looked for that split-second.

You see yellow-collared dudes, probably the security dudes, coming at Shelby and you from the crowds.

"Oh shit!" laughs Shelby. "Run!" She pulls on you.

You both run, at first dropping off the stage, then pushing away people, heading away toward the overhangs that lead toward Panera.

You run. You run your ass off, boy, and you look behind yourself and see these men chasing after both you and Shelby. She is leading the way. "Run!" she says.

You cut the corner of Panera and cross the street. Taxi drivers stop abrupt and spin (not really) out of control, honking, blaring horns. SUVs stop. Everyone on the road stops.

Shelby is just laughing away. Jolly, jolly.

You get to the other side of the street, going up the outdoor escalators that lead up to Muvico, the theater, and Shelby says, "Lets go see a movie! They won't see up there!" but you don't wanna do that because a movie is just burning time for you.

So you say, "Nah, lets go beachin'."

This suffices for Shelby. She nods.

You look at—

2:43 P.M.

Shelby and you walk down the other staircase on the other side of Muvico and Shelby asks you where in the hell Rob is.

You tell her, "I don't know."

"Fiddlesticks," she says.

"What a weirdo thing to say." You grin.

"Where's your car, _______?"

"You're the one who's got the ticket, doll-face."

"Crap . . . I'm high, I forgot."

"Naturally."

"Oh hush, estúpido."

"Bleh!" You feel like you're lightening up.

"I love you, _______." This is the first time a chick has said this to you. She bats those eyes of hers. Says, "You're funny, sweetums. . . ."

2:49 P.M.

Both of you finally get to valet and the valet boy finds your car and brings you it and you pay him, irritated because Shelby didn't pay like she said she would, but she just blinks at you and says, "Aww, you love me, sweet'ums" and this makes you have butterflies, even though you promised yourself in the past that you would never, ever have a chick run over you or make you feel like she runs shit, but you guess that's completely thrown out the window when the reality of the situation is that she actually does in fact run shit. Though you both get into your car, Shelby asks you, "Beach? Really?" and you say, "Yeah, yeah, been wanting to today," and she goes on, like, "But I go all the time! The beach is hella boring. I'm already tan," and you respond to that, by saying, "I'm paler than an F-ing ghost," and she giggles while saying, "Yeah, babe, but I wanna chill!" and you think she is completely adorable. Then you start driving down Daytura, which is a street over from both your old job and her current job, and she goes, "Lets have some hookah!" "Later," you say. "Okay, sweetums," she says back. Then you say, "Who run it?" "You," she goes. And you drive over the bridge after you pass Trinity Road, and you go into Palm Beach, the richest F-ing place ever, where Opera spends her summers, where James Patterson, great a lovely awesome bullshit author guy, lives and works, and you go all the way to the end of the street and see the beach, empty as all hells give. You find parking, even though you shouldn't've. "You run it," Shelby says, smiling her bright-white smile. Awesomeness. Out. Ouch. Burn. Feet. Walk. There. Ocean.

3:01 P.M.

Beach is pretty pretty, you think, but as you walk on the cement, looking at the beach's horizon, Shelby attempts to hold your hand, but you hesitate, embarrassed, because you never thought a chick would initiate something like this, something that is odd to you, that is super emotional, with its pure compassion, and so you hesitate because you're not used to physical affection with chicks, with anyone for that matter, and Shelby eyes you, concerned, asking, "What's wrong, babe? No touchy? I like you, just so you know, it's okay," and this motherly move moves you into complying. So you finally hold her hand and she grins a type of grin you get when you open up a present and it's the one thing you love and crave most, this sense of love. As you two walk down the sidewalk, cutting into an open space in the wall, striding down the hot, crunchy sand that burns the pads of your feety feet slightly, the sand going all between your toes with Shelby gripping you tighter during this and going all "ouch ouch ouch," you both finally get to the edge of the ocean and the smell is so tropical that it sets a wave of endorphins exploding throughout your mind because it's the one fantasy that you have always wanted, the chick and you together on a F-ing beachy beach. So you and Shelby settle for a bit, sitting down, looking off into the horizon, smiling, squinting too, towel-less, utterly hyped on life, and Shelby turns to you, looks at you, into you, and approves of you, then goes into her pocket and pulls out her phone, going into the old iTunes app and playing the song "First Day Of My Life" by Bright Eyes, and you think it's hella corny because this would obviously mean that she is a girly girl to put on such a lovey-dovey song for this extravaganza you two are right now having, but you grin and also think it's cute and you appreciate everything she's doing for you. She sits closer, leaning her head on your shoulder, and you feel like a total bowse slash king for a sec, so you turn to her and ask, "Shelby, can I ask you a question?" She goes, "Yeah, baby, anything, shoot." "Okay," you go back, "I just want you to know that I'm a virgin." "Really?" she says, more surprise than you expect. "Wow. . . . I mean, that's okay. I am too," but her eyes shift to the left, which you have heard before means that someone is lying and trying to make up something from the more "creative" part of the brain. You don't believe this, so you say, "I don't believe this," and Shelby goes, "I swear," and you go, "Wow," and she goes, "Yeah, yeah, but what did you wanna ask?" and so you ask, "I wanted to ask you if you'd have sex with me, but before you say no, I just want you to know that it's not because I want to kill your personal space or be a player, it's because I really have liked you for a long time and today is, uh, a special day . . . um, um . . ." You stop. You don't want to tell her about your little plan to kill yourself by next afternoon, so you say, instead, "Nevermind, forget it," and Shelby goes, "I'm kind of bummed you'd ask such a thing. I thought you were different," and then you assure her that you are in fact different, and you are not just trying to get into her pants, but she does not understand, considering she thinks you will be alive longer than just a couple of hours—go figure, naturally—so she says, "I think I'll go now. It was awesome hanging with you for a bit, but I really gotta go." "No, please, no," you say. "I'm sorry. We don't have to." "Did you ever consider about having a condom before asking?" she says. "Because that'd be inconsiderate of you to not have one before asking." "Umm, I'm just . . . Sorry," you say, so depressed you can hardly breathe. "I'll leave. You enjoy the beach." She doesn't say anything, just nods. So you get up and walk walk walk up the beach and back up to the streets and go back into your car, sitting on in, and you decide to call Rob because he is probably having the time of his life, considering that's all he does because he doesn't give a flying *bleh!*, and he promised you that he'd provide you with one of those "good times," too. So you pull out your phone and notice . . .

3:18 P.M.

While you wait for Rob to answer his phone, the sounds of dialing booms in your eardrum, but while this happens you're pondering this overwhelming idea of hatred you have: the fact that you have perpetual feelings of depression, and this depression is linked to you not knowing what you want in life. You always feel "on-edge" or "waiting for something," and it's severely annoying. It's like a crackhead losing his memory of the last two years of his life but he started smoking crack a year ago.

He doesn't remember smoking crack, but he's craving something; something sweet, but he doesn't know what it is. He just searches. That's the feeling you've had for your twenty-one years you have lived on this planet. That's what it's like. This feeling that you want to get a need satisfied but you do not know what the need is.

Finally, Rob answers, going like, "What's up, cool cat?!"

You ask him, "Why, dude? Why is it that I'm such a screw-up? Why can't I enjoy anything in life? Why?!" You're hysterical, crying, the tears just keep rushing out and you know it's been built up for such a long time.

Rob sighs. "Bro, calm . . . down . . . now. I've never met anyone in my life who is such a Debbie-downer."

You tell him the whole crackhead idea you were just thinking about, in detail.

"You're insane," he says after it. "The only people who wouldn't think that that's not insane are people that are insane." He laughs. "Bro, meet me at Muvico."

"Okay, whatever," you're like.

3:23 P.M.

A cop car is following you while you go ten miles-per-hour over the speed limit heading down back to City Place. But you cut a left into Rosemary at the intersection and the cop keeps going down Okeechobee, like the lil' bitch he is, you think, and you're like, "Woo. Close call."

Takes you no time to find parking in the parking garage across from Muvico, and though you do in fact find parking right next to the motorcycle parking, the closest to the entrance, you feel like, damn, women are lame for convincing you to do this or that, more specifically with the valet parking thingama-bob.

You get out of your car but don't feel like looking at your phone or watch because you don't want to know the time. At this point you just want the day to end.

You walk down the street and two girlies stare at you, one being all close to the other, and she is all goggly-eyed about you as she passes you and you briefly hear a murmur she does under her breath, saying, Wow, look at *him*, and this vaguely makes you think that they think you're ugly, but also you think that maybe normal people would think that she maybe likes you. Whatever, you seem to say to yourself.

Your phone rings in your pocket while you're still walking, about to go into Sunglass Hut, so you press one of the volume buttons from outside your pocket, like the genius you are, and it silences it. You go into Sunglass Hut.

You see a bunch of black Wayfarer Raybans and you try them on, each, in a row, and then, tap tap taping your shoulder, an old—no, scratch that—a hottie, um, asks you, "Can I help you with something, hun?"

"No. Just browsing. Thanks." You think this is *so* awkward.

"Those look great on you, just FYI." She smiles.

"Hey," you say, all like a questioning cop, "I have a question for you."

"Yes . . . ?"

"I tend to have this problem with women. I feel like I can only meet them by accident. Like right now. How you're coming up to *me* and now *we* are conversing and maybe becoming friends."

She squints. "Well . . . I think you shouldn't feel that way. Me, for example, I, um, just go up to people and say whatever I'd like to say to them. If they take it, great, but if not, whatever, no skin off my bone."

"You see, I envy that you are able to do that. For a long time I've just been afraid of chicks. Particularly ones I like or find attractive."

"But why?" this brunette, big tits, wide hips, little waist, business suit with the short skirt that you wouldn't mind taking off, asks. "You seem really so confident."

"Do you really mean that? Or are you just trying to make me feel good to get a sale . . . to get a commission?"

She laughs a bit awkwardly. "No no *no*, I'd never!" she lies. "I actually thought you looked pretty cute in those shades and I wanted to compliment you."

After thinking for a sec, you go, "Do you think women would find me attractive? You know, if I just muster up the courage to speak and not be such a pussy?"

"You did with me. If I wasn't at work and you asked me out, I'd go in a heartbeat."

You smile. "Thanks, lovey."

"No, thank you—my pleasure," the hottie is like.

You scratch your head. "Er, this is when I lose things to talk about."

"It's okay. I do havta get back to work." A couple, looking rich, comes in through the door. "Cya, stud," the hottie concludes. She turns around.

You smile.

She goes up to the couple as they browse, going up to the male as he looks at some Oakley's, and she says to him, "Can I help you with something, hun?" then, shortly after, "Those look great on you, just FYI," and this enrages you.

As you pass out the door, you yell to the hottie, "SCREW YOU!" and she looks startled, all jumpy, the couple too, but you turn around, not caring, and you go out into the bright, bright streets.

You pull out your phone, it's ringing. . . . Robby. Oh, and you see the time too.

3:34 P.M.

Around the corner of Sunglass Hut is a staircase that leads up to Muvico. You go up that.

Rob asks you on the phone, "Where you at?"

"Was at Sunglass Hut."

"Come to Muvico."

"I'll be there in a jiff."

"A *jiff*?"

"Just . . . *ugh!* nevermind! I'll be there!" And you hang up.

You step up the stairs and hold onto the handles and feel anxiety rushing over you, but it won't last long. This will end soon.

You look up the stairs and at the very top is Rob with his hands in his pockets, with a grin on his face, and you finally get up the stairs and give him dap, like a G, and he tells you that you missed out on something hella dope.

"What was it?" you ask, curious.

"You missed out. These Redbull girls stopped by after you and Shelby were doing your little dancin' thing, and I got one of their numbers. They told me that there's a party at Dr. Feel-Goods or whatever."

"So what did I miss?" squints you.

"If you could've seen these chicks, you'd *know* what you missed," Rob elaborates.

"Oh."

"Anyway, where d'you wanna go?"

After a seven-second pause, you say, "I wanna get laid somehow, someway."

Rob grins, saying, "I know a place. How much cash you got?"

"Like a couple hundred," you kinda sorta lie. "Didn't ever pay rent, sort of."

"Cool, perfect. I know just the place. Come on." He turns and starts walking.

" 'Kay," you sigh, following him. More walking. *Crap!* Not rock on.

3:41 P.M.

Down Rosemary, all the way down, passed City Place, about just before Tamron, the most ghetto-est ghetto of all ghettos, right after passing the Publix market, you and Rob both see a massage parlor by the name of Madam Frances' Fantasy Parlor, which, *duh!* couldn't be more blatantly *obvious*, but whatever, you roll with it. It's your last day, whatever.

"Dude," Rob says to you, "get ready. Been here once. These girls are *nuts*."

"Oh . . . okay."

You get up to the entrance and it looks like a regular house, a porch and everything, but has a sign that says the name of the place in spray-painted cursive, all girly and pink and whatnot.

Rob knocks on the entrance.

"Dude dude dude," he says, hyped, *"fuhhh!"*

You roll your eyes.

"Ello, lovey," a really overly feminine voice says behind the door, the voice also sounding quite Asian. "One *meen*-it."

"Oh, this outta be good," Rob says.

You and him step back two meters.

The door swings out, flying, hitting the wall, and an absolutely haggard Asian lady greets you, saying, "Well, *'ello*, loveys!" and she has her stockings on, her robe and everything, and this makes you go wide-eyed because you've never seen some shit like this.

You turn to Rob and he's lovin' it completely, "and *gooooood* day to you!" he says in such a masculine, lame-player voice that annoys the hell out of you.

"Thaz good!" the Asian lady says. She turns to you. "Oh my! So *hand*some! What's yu name, sho-gar?"

"Don't worry 'bout it," you say. "I got business to attend to."

"Oh my! Get ri' tu et, I see! I *see!* Well, come on *een!*" She steps back and waves her hand in to sign that, yes, it's okay for you creepers to come inside. . . . Money talks, bullshit walks.

The place smells like a gym locker-room masked with Frebreeze and other smells that are probably perfume-based. There's a desk with some secretary in a robe and there's a line of girls against the wall, all hotties that you wouldn't mind showing off to the old parents.

Rob kind of limps like a G over to the desk and you just roll your eyes at how he's acting. But he says to the secretary-looking chick, "One each, please," and she goes, "Okay, hun."

Clearing your throat, you say, "Eh-*hem*, I want two."

Rob turns around and raises his eyebrows. "Yeah right, kid."

"I don't give a crap," you say to him.

He laughs, turning back around, saying to the secretary, "Two each."

"Okay," she says, giggling after.

You and Rob turn around and look at the line of girls, all having something wrong in the fantasy you have of this extravaganza: her tits too small; hers too big; her legs too wide; her thighs too fat; her waist too skinny; her waist too wide; her hips too thick; her lips too whatever, whatever . . .

Rob goes, "Bro, that's screwed-up," and you realize that you actually said these opinions out loud.

"Sorry . . . ?" you say to all the chicks.

They don't say a word, they just look at you like a task or a job to do, no pleasure involved.

The entrance lady asks you, "Which one?"

You go, "Any. I don't care," because you really, in fact, don't give a flying *bleh!*

"Okay. Go in dee back room"—she points to it—"and I'll have two see yu."

" 'Kay." You walk toward it. Rob follows.

As you enter passed the hanging beads over the entrance, Rob asks you, "Yo, why are you being such a dick to 'em?"

"Because they have a friggin' job ta do."

"You're suppose to be havin' fun."

"Whatever." You're just over it, you guess.

"That's all you ever say. Listen. I'm going to the other room out there. Peace."

"Okay," you say.

He leaves.

It's pretty F-ing quiet, so you sit down on the huge lone bed that's there and you reach into your pocket and bring out your phone, seeing:

3:59 P.M.

Two chicks come in, both Asian, the one with tits too big and the one with tits too small, and so you sigh, but not because of them being inadequate but because you're really not too hyped on losing the old V card to a bunch of scalawags. You look up and see an intercom on the ceiling. The two chicks step closer, close together, and this makes you nervous as hell, but then they end up on either side of you, holding you, caressing you, giggling, and then you effortlessly fall down and bounce on the sheets, your feet still on the ground at the end of the bed, and you put your hands behind your head, acting tough but really scared, and while some music, probably some sensual Drake song with hella auto-tune, starts to play on the intercom, the two chicks, in unison, say, "You iz a pretty white boy," and then, looking at each other, "Jinx! You owe meh a sodah!" and they just laugh like hyenas and this kinda makes you smirk just a little bit. "White boi, you iz cute!" They start laying on top of you, legs over each of your legs, palms on biceps, and you start to get a hard-on that towers in your pants. One of them reaches down, feeling it. She goes, "Oh my!" "Yeah," you go back, "um, this is weird." "Why?" both the Asian babes say in unison again. "I'm, uhh, kind of a, uhh, virgin," you say. Their eyes just light up. One of them starts trying to take off your belt, unzipping you. "How?" one of them says. "How een de world could yu keep that? How old arrr yu?" "I don't know," you say. "Twenty-one." "Oh wow," the other Asian chick, the one unzipping you, says. "I see, I see." You start to squirm. This is not right. You scurry up more on top of the bed, knees up, scared, and you blurt, "Stop!" The girls look at you like an alien, saying, "Whazz wrong?" "I just don't know," you say. "Can't we just talk?" "But you said that you wanted two girlies, like us," the un-zipper Asian chick says. "We better be still gettin' paid if yu tu chic . . . chic*ken,* as you Amerikanz say." "No," you're like. "Nah, I just wanna talk about you guys and how you became hoes and how you were treated in the past and how you ended up with a job like this and how your education was and if you were born into a good family and if it is really true that chicks like you almost always have had daddy issues and if that's true and if you never were a hoe would you consider dating a dude like me and if I am adequate enough and if your job is hard to do and if the dudes treat you bad and if you were ever considering just going to college or having kids or settling down or becoming somebodies or anything at all that is positive or if you even are positive to begin with or if you are negative like Yours Truly or if this all makes sense or when you guys lost your V cards and if you would lose them to hoes or if I'm a dumbass or if this is all just one big cry for help or if I'm not something to be loved or if I'm just . . . I'm just . . ." You stop. You start to cry with your head buried in your hands. You feel like you're nothing. You feel like nothing in this world can help you. The un-zipper Asian chick says, "Why yu care?" You go, " 'Cause." " 'Cause why?" she asks. " 'Cause I'mma 'bout ta die in a couple hours." In unison (you are starting to think they are F-ing twins with the amount of jinxes they do) the Asian chicks say, "What?" Yeah, whatever, nevermind nevermind. You get up, depressed as all hell, and, sitting at the edge of the posh posh bed, you tie your shoes tight because they loosened somehow, someway, and you stand up after, then turn to the lovely, lovely hookers that are lying together on the bed, and you wave at them, awkwardly, and they feel that it is in fact awkward, so you start to step backward, tippy-toeing, and then you suddenly turn around and bolt out the F-ing pathway with the damn beads hanging. You turn the corner, where another room is, and you hope Rob is in there, not getting head, though you think that's un-homie of you to think that. You go in and, sure as hell, there's two Asian hardbodies with Rob, one on the bed's edge touching Rob's pecks as he stands in front of her with his back to her, shirtless, and the other one on her knees, chicken-heading and gobbling down on his meat-stick. But you don't care, you just say, "Lets F-ing go, yo!" and as you say this, Rob, coming back to reality from moments ago losing himself to the best thing a man can do, looks at you and blurts, "AH, BRO!" and this makes you laugh. He pushes these bitches out the way and pulls his pants up and runs out the room with you, tugging at your shirt's collar, angry and blue-balled, and this, again, makes you laugh harder, and then, as you go out into the open, outside, the headmaster of the hooker station you just left at yells that you both need to pay for the services you just apparently walked out on. But you and Rob run down the street, giggling like morons, and you look down at your watch, thinking what a day what a day.

4:31 P.M.

Guess who calls you. Here's a hint: She's hot and you just met her about three hours ago and she totally got offended when you asked her to sex you, even though you both just met. . . . Yup, Shelby. You pick up the phone, bummed that she's calling, and you answer, very monotone, "Yeah?" and she goes, "Where are you?!" "I'm heading down Rosemary with Rob," you say, the voice of Rob, you think, probably in the background on her line going, "Hell yeah hell yeah hell yeah, we are bowse, niggie," because on your end of the spectrum, next to you, he's pretty much shouting this while you both walk down this street you guys are at. "Oh," Shelby says. "Listen. I'm sorry about, um, rejecting you, babe. I'm just not used to guys being so straightforw—" The line drops. You look on your phone's screen. The satellite bars are showing a big, big X. Your phone company just disconnected you. You go into the generic text app, whatever, and you text Shelby:

Hey, phoen got turend off.

You send it, then, correcting, you text another thing like:

turned* phone*

And, seconds, she texts back like:

it's ok. I was gonna say that i should rethink the idea of sex with you you're awesome and i should do it.

This makes you roll your eyes because you think she couldn't be serious, not at all. You text like:

Oh.

And, quicker than you expect, she texts:

Where r u?

You go:

Meet at Starbucks

Faster, she goes:

K<3

You put your phone back into your pocket because you're losing whatever wifi connection you just now had. Rob is still hyped on the hookers.

"Woo! Hell yes!"

You roll your eyes. Clocky clock.

4:50 P.M.

Rob is behind you, asking, "Why we goin' to StaryBuck-Buck?"

You answer with, "Because."

"Because why?"

"Because Shelby is there. We're meetin' up."

Rob touches your shoulder, face to face with you, being all grinny. "Not a way to spend time on your last hours, broseph," he says.

You sigh, "She, uh, wants to, uh, have sexy time."

"Oh my!" Rob goes, sarcastic. "My niggie ri' here."

You grin. "Shut up."

"I'll go, yo, if you want."

"Nah, be with me. You're my escape route."

"Okay, my niggie."

More walking.

4:55 P.M.

"We're here," Rob says. "Where's she?"

"Don't know," you say.

Rob looks around.

You go, "Maybe she's—"

"There!" Rob blurts, pointing. "Over there!" He goes behind you, pushes you along. "Go get 'er," he laughs.

Shelby is sitting there, alone, kinda over it, obviously waiting for some kind of handsome devil to sweep her up from her sit session, give her a good time, love her, hold her, be with her, and these thoughts run through your head up until you are in front of her finally, with Rob behind you friggin' gigglin' like a damn madman.

"Hey," Shelby says to you, standing up.

"Hey." You feel awk.

"I'll leave you two alone," Rob says, then walks on off. This makes you roll your eyes because it indicates obviously that you told him she wants to have sex.

"So . . . sex . . . ?" she starts.

"Uhh," you sigh, unsure. "You sure?"

"Sit with me for a minute, please." She sits down.

You do too.

"So," she says to you, across from you, eyes on you, into you, staring, goggly-eyed, awesomeness, "why do you want to?"

"Umm, is this a trick question?"

"No, silly-willy, a girl's gotta know." She smiles.

"Why are you down all of a sudden?" You squint. "This is weird of a chick to do."

"Listen." She rests her elbow on the damn table. "I just . . . I don't know, you seem . . . different. You know?"

You put your elbows on the table too, all sighing, "So . . . you like me?"

"Yes yes." She unconsciously bats her eyes. "You seem really awesome."

"I'm not. Seriously." Your face feels numb.

"Why so glum?" Shelby's head tints.

"I have issues."

"Like what? We all do, you know."

"But mine are . . . different."

"How?" She squints.

"I look at life like a thing you just, I don't know, do."

"Know whatcha mean." Her hands drop and touch the table's top, she crosses her arms.

"I think everyone is just . . . you know, living this life and just, uh, trying to survive it," you say. "I don't even know why I'm here, frankly."

"I just wanted to know why you like me," doll-face says. Her hand touches yours.

"Yes," you sigh, "I know, but, um, you gotta know a few things. I'm an insecure person. I worry a lot. I like you for, um, your looks really. I never met you, so I don't think there was any other reason. Now I'm thinking it's screwed-up of me to be liking you, maybe."

Shelby goes, "But you said all those nice things at my house today. You had so much to say about me. What about *those* things?"

"Maybe, um, maybe I was just trying to impress you. Maybe I'm just another asshole asking for, uh, sex."

"Look. Do you know what I was doing before you arrived at my doorstep?"

You ask, "What were you doing?" but think, Hope it involved an idea of me, yo.

She answers, "I was being texted by some other guys. You see, at the hookah bar, they pretty much hired me because of my looks."

You grin. "Naturally."

"Yes"—Shelby's smile—"naturally. And so I'm up there working and I get hit on by lots of guys. I mean these total creepers have asked me the weirdest shit. One guy asked me to massage his feet or whatever and he would pay extra. So gross, dude."

"Wow." Your eyes go wide. And you're thinking, What kind of bar is this? what kind of people are there? why would they ask such a random thing?

"Yeah, I know. Some other night I got asked by, like, *twelve* different guys if they could have my number. Five of which were cool and I gave 'em it—not gonna lie—and they all texted me back the next day. Most of them I don't even respond to. Hate the idea of meeting a guy like that."

"Dude, I'm a guy who showed up at your house," you remind her cute self, "who you've never met."

"Yeah, but . . . I don't know, you're different."

"You keep saying this but I'm having a hard time finding out why."

She holds your hands tight. "Okay, remember that one day, the day your pizza place had that old lady out front who got her purse stolen right in front of her?"

This idea has never came up, but you oddly remember it.

"Well, I do," Shelby keeps going on and on to you, even though you didn't answer the question. "The scumbag came up while she was eating and took her damn bag. I saw him running across the street and yellin' 'n' shit and you chased him and tackled his ass." Wow, Shelby doesn't seem like such a goodie-two-shoes anymore.

Makes you laugh. "Yeah, I remember that! *Ha!* But what about it?"

"What guy does that?!" Shelby is laughing too. "I mean, to have the damn *balls* to do that! Not only was it sweet but it took guts. Hun, you say you have issues—I know, I get that—but I think your issues outweigh who you are. You seem like a go-getter. That's what leads me to what I was doin' at my house before you came. I was getting basically harassed by dudes over text-message to chill or to hang or to straight-up make out, whatever. And I thought, you know, I really wish a guy would just get off his lazy ass and just be man enough to take charge and tell me what to do."

You ask, "But isn't that, um, rape?"

Shelby laughs. "No silly! No way. Not like that, silly. I mean in the sense of taking charge. That's a real man. I want a man that will just come up to me and say exactly what's on his mind and not beat around the bush and just do something about it. That's a real man. And that, my darling wittle ferret lover, is you!" Huh?

This hits your stomach so hard that you feel sick with butterflies.

"You okay?" Shelby asks sweetly. "Hope I'm not making you feel uncomfortable, boo."

"You're not," you say. "Not at all. I just . . . I don't know. That's just everything I've always wanted to be. I'm so happy I left a good impression onto you."

"Well, the reason I said no to your sexual offer at the beach was because I just thought of the men that have done that, so I got into bitch-mode, kind of . . . Sorry."

"Yeah." You nod. "I know, I know. That's why I left. Felt like I screwed-up."

"You didn't at all. I just didn't know how to respond. But dude, I wanna—"

"I love that you say the word 'dude.' It's sexy," you interrupt, grin grinnin'. "I never hear chicks say that. They're always reserved and never straight-forward."

Shelby grins, too, and says, "Oh hush, silly. But yeah, anyway, I do wanna do sex with ya. But I just wanna know why you want to. I want to hear your thoughts."

"Well, as you know, I'm a virgin and—"

"Yeah," Shelby interrupts, "what's up with that? How are you one?"

"I guess . . . just've always been iffy about girls."

"Are you gay, maybe?"

You rub your eyebrows. "Always asked that—no, I'm not."

"Oh."

"I just . . ." You stop. You hold your head. "I guess I'm just waiting . . . or looking."

"Looking for . . . ?"

"I guess . . . maybe I'm just scared of women."

"Why?"

"Whenever I see a girl I like, one that is usually good-looking, I tense up and cower down and just let her, uh, go. I'm scared of her, maybe."

"You're scared of rejection?"

"No."

"Then what is it?"

"I guess I just feel unreal."

"Huh?"

"I feel like I don't deserve it. I spend all my time looking to find this one moment where I can be a somebody for a girl. I spend all this time getting work and jobs and everything and I just get disappointed in the end. So, you see, I look at, um, the girl, this hot mama girlie girl, and I just see myself not with her. It's almost fictional. I see her as something that is just simply unobtainable. This happens with my everyday life. I feel like I'm just a blur. Nothing feels like it works. My head always hurts, I cry over shit alone, I feel like I'm just doing the same ole shit over and over again. And this all sucks."

Shelby looks at you with this sympathy that almost sickens you. And then she says, "I feel bad. I feel like you shouldn't feel that way about life or yourself."

You say, "More people look highly of me than I do myself."

"What?"

"I mean, um, people think more highly of me than I do myself."

"But you're a great person. I think you don't give yourself enough credit."

"I feel like I don't deserve credit. Success makes me sick to my stomach, always."

"I've never heard that from someone."

"Well, look. This one time in highschool my parents were always nagging me about grades 'n' shit, trying to get me to do better. At one point my mom said, 'If you get just a C and some Ds in your classes, I'll pay you.' "

Shelby looks baffled. "That's . . . wrong, hun."

"Thing of it is is that whenever I got an A and they were proud of me, I would feel sick to my stomach and the A wouldn't feel good for me. But when I got an F, and when they would scold me, take shit away, do all that, I felt more comfortable. This idea is why I didn't talk to you, this same principal. Look. I would totally talk to you and be the best boyfriend ever, but I would feel sick and on-edge all the time because I wouldn't be comfortable. In a way, I like being unsuccessful. It's all I know. My brain is telling me to go that route."

Shelby squints like crazy to you, asking, "You're so weird. Never heard this."

You go, "Because you said that, I feel less sick."

"That's . . . just so . . . *wrong.*"

"I just hate my life really."

"We gotta change that."

"No time."

"Why?"

"I'm dying in a couple hours. Today's my last day."

"Last day?" She leans more forward. "What do you mean?"

"Twenty-four hours to live."

"What's wrong with you?"

"Uh—"

"Cancer?" she blurts, questioning.

Pause.

"*Sure*," you sigh, thinking, Whatever floats your boat, doll-face.

"Oh shit, *wow!* No *wonder* you've been doing stuff now of all times." She gets up, scoots her chair over next to you, sits, hugs you, says, "This sucks, boo," and she starts to slightly cry into your shoulder, not a lot but enough to be kind of a big deal.

You think that you totally lied to her and this kind of makes you feel like a total scumbag, but you hold onto her anyway because your suicide is a selfish act with selfish consequences that can't and shouldn't be taken lightly, but whatever, you roll with it anyway, considering that you want to have the best last day ever. From around her shoulder, looking down, you see your watch.

5:14 P.M.

"Hey," Shelby says, her eyes red and wet, sniffling after, pause. "Tell you what." Sniffles. "Lets just have the best day ever. I think we all should live life like it's our last."

You ask, "So the saying 'live life everyday like it's your last' has some actual meaning?"

"Yeah." Sniffles. "But I wanna utilize that saying more."

You squint. "Well, um, what do you wanna do?"

"Don't know. What were your plans, hun?"

"Really, my only plan was you."

"You only wanted to talk with *me?*"

"Yeah."

"Confess your liking of me?"

You nod. "Mhm."

"You're a sap!" She sticks her tongue out at you.

"I know." You grin. "Yes." Nod.

"We should go WILD!"

"How so?"

Shelby gives this look, this suggestive look with her eyebrow up, flick flick, and she un-hugs you, gets up, pulls her chair out, one foot up, step up, one foot up again, on table now, and stands up, full up, clapping, shouting, "What a lovely day, people! You all should get up from your phones and start havin' some fun!"

This makes you grin.

She stops, looks down at you, whispers, "Come on, get up here, lovey," hand all held out to you or whatever.

You grab it and step one foot up, yada yada, just like Shelby did, and you stand up on the table, but, weirdly, as you get up, you see in the window of Starbucks the blondie who you totally and randomly asked to make out with you, even though she has a made-up boyfriend named Greg.

The blondie is looking at you through the window and she is smiling, eyes all awesome, and others in her line are like "wow" too.

You stand full up there, right there on the table, dazed, confused, and Shelby slings her arm around your shoulders, like a bro, and shouts to everyone, "Lets party! Screw it! WOO!" and she starts dancing with you.

A lady, white, mid-forties, flower-printed shirt, off in the crowd, starts to dance with her husband, also being old, all that.

This makes a . . .

. . . chain reaction.

. . . *Clap* . . . *clap* . . . *clap* to the beat.

Strangely, weirdly, whatever, a Mexican whatever band, you think it's called a "mariachi," comes up, rolls up, instruments in hand, *boo-bee-boo-bee*, singing some crazy music.

Everyone . . . is . . . here . . . clapping.

You say to Shelby as she's bumping her bum bum into you, like before, "Hey, um, this is weird for me. I . . . I, um . . ."

She turns around, grabs your hands, moves you along with her, effortlessly, gracefully, and this weird butterfly feeling hits your head, just like when you were in Elementary school and you would feel good whenever you did something right. No words said. Everything feels slow-motion. You finally understand what getting over fear is . . . kind of. Not quite.

5:30 P.M.

Oh . . . my . . . *God*, you think. Looking away from your watch, you notice it's already five-thirty and you know the sun is looking all setting 'n' shit and the sky is starting to get to be light bluish tint, even though Summer is close. Or maybe you're just trippin'.

Everyone is being loud because everyone is now dancing as couples and it's all one big happy fiesta.

You ask, still holding and dancing with Shelby, "Ayo, lets do more shit!"

"Like what?" she's saying, arms up, moving hips. "Lets keep dancing."

"Lets go to a club."

"Okay."

Silence between you guys for a sec.

"AYO!" a voice yells.

You turn and look down, puzzled, then, startlingly happy, you see Rob, the blonde barista in his right arm, and, laughing like hell, he goes, "Wha-wha-ha-ha-ha-t the fuh-uh-uhck are you two do-o-in'?!" He keeps laughing and the blondie is laughing too. "Wow, man! Classic. Love it. Lightening up, niggie!"

You nod, grin grin.

Shelby asks Rob, "Who's this?" pointing at the blondie.

"Met her. She dopeski. Ordered some coffee and she wanted to tag along. Her name's Connie."

"Hi," you say to her.

"Hi." She's suddenly batting her eyes, briefly.

Shelby catches this. She pulls you in, not showing her jealously clearly, but everyone knows it's there.

"Well, uh . . ." Rob starts, "what's up, guys? What we doin'?"

"Lets go to a club!" you say wildly, all hyped but slightly innocently.

"I got a better idea," Connie says.

Y'all turn to her.

"There's a big party down in Lake Worth, near my house, and I was invited. I'm sure you guys could go too. Wanna?"

"Hell yes," Rob and you say at the same exact time.

"I'm not sure," Shelby disagrees. You feel her tightening her grip on you. "Lake Worth parties are nuts. Last one I went to, a huge fight broke out, I got my hair pulled, and I didn't even drink because nobody brought any beer. They just drank it all."

"This one's fine," Connie says. "Trust me. It's all only homies."

You think this is a stupid thing or comment for her to say because how "homie only" could it be when she's inviting you three, Shelby and you and Rob, complete strangers, to the party.

"Lets do it," you say. Follow. Walk. Talk. Shit.

5:46 P.M.

You're walking walking walking with Shelby and Connie and Rob next to you and Shelby asks you, close to your ear, "Hey, do you trust this Connie girl?" and you answer with, "No," and she goes, "Oh. Okay. 'Cause I don't either. Watch yourself. We'll hit this swareé for a bit, then go off to some clubs. Then, just maybe if you're lucky, we'll do some lovin'. Deal?" Smile. "Okay," you say, whatever. Silence. More walking.

5:51 P.M.

Connie's car is parked wayyyyyy the hell over there, deep in the parking garage, and you all four just walk, but then Rob says, "Race you niggies to the car" while Connie presses her car alarm button and makes hella noise. You all run and everyone's all smiley, yeah, but you feel depressed about something. Maybe it's the fact that you feel like this is ending too soon. Or the fact that when you make something, it's over, gone. Or the idea that when you make something that you've worked on for months, nobody even cares. Then you think that maybe this whole plan of yours is going to end up the same: Nobody will care. But then a little voice inside your head, probably your subconscious, says, "It's okay. You're going to leave soon," and suddenly all the depression goes away and everything feels more enjoyable, so you run faster than everyone else and eventually run and place your hand, first place, on the car's trunk, huffing and puffing after, and then Shelby, her cute self, puts her hand on the trunk too, second place, and she looks at you, huffing and puffing too, like you, and grins, asking you, "Why are you making that face?" The reason you're making a kind of monotone-ish, screwtard face is because the same idea of nobody caring has, again, swooped over your goddamn noggin'. Shelby comes closer to you, as you stand silent to her question, and she kisses you, saying after, "It's okay. This party will be over soon, promise," and then you feel happy, once again. Four in the car . . . right about . . . NOW!

6:01 P.M.

Blasting the shit out of some mother-F-ing Pink Floyd, the song "Us And Them," Connie revs her engine after there's a bright green light flashing after a red light, indicating to go, *screwtard!* and she looks sternly at the road, and though you're thinking that she is just tryna impress you guys and she really doesn't do this on normal occasions, Rob is yelling, "Hell yes, niggie!" at the top of his F-ing lungs while Shelby, more bored out of her mind than you are, leans back into her seat, holding onto the back of Rob's seat, and she looks out the window, over it. As you notice all of this, you tune it out and look out your side's window too. You shut your eyes, thinking about Pink Floyd's music and trying to figure out its true meaning of how they say in the end it's always round and round, and round, and then you think about how that's so true because obviously you're an organism that's just a duplicate of your parents and now you're in the world, not from choice, and you have to deal with it. So now the end is going to be round and round, even though maybe you personally think, Who screwed with nothingness? Then your brain rants on about going to the top of—

"Are you okay?" you seem to hear Shelby saying to you, cutting off your thoughts. . . . "Were you napping?"

You open your eyes and turn to her. "Yeah."

She holds your hand, snapping you out of your little head coma, and she says, "I really do love you, I think."

"Oh," you say, "you don't say. . . ."

"You just overthink a lot and it scares me."

Scares lots of people. They will soon see.

Oh, look, a bird . . . a watch.

6:18 P.M.

Sweet, sweet Connie baby rides up down Congress then turns left and speeds down Lake Worth, passed Lake Worth Highschool, blaring techno, and y'all jump up and down in the car, even as she flies over speed bumps that makes you guys bump your heads on the roof slightly. You're happy, yeah, but it's gonna end soon enough, you think, yet again, and it's getting F-ing old. Just cheer the F up, screwtard. Connie scoots into the gas station next to Rita's Ice Cream and she says to the window guy, "Thirty-two pack of Miller lights, please," all like a G and whatnot, and though you totally *hate* Miller light and Bud light and any other beer that's not Dos Equis, Rob goes, "Yes. Hell yes," because it's his fav, next to Corona and, of course, Bud light. Couple seconds of waiting and talking about a debate on the differences between our solar system's distance to the universe's ratio distance between the galaxies, which you think is completely absurd but everyone in the car thinks it's probably the same, the window guy comes back with the magical potion in aluminum cans and tells Connie, "Tank you come again," all indian as all fork, then Connie speeds off and doesn't say a goddam word to him, but he shuts his window doors, whatever-like. And you probably think that he's probably treated like that all the time and he thinks of us Americans as stuck-up assholes and whatever, whatever. And you look out the window and see palms and hear everyone in the car talk about something blurred, but then you glance at your watch and see it reads

6:29 P.M.

but everything feels totally artificial, for some odd, lame reason.

"It's too early to be going to a party," you say.

Connie, still looking at the road, says, "We aren't."

"Then where?" Shelby asks, suddenly surprised. "I knew not the party, but where?"

"No party right meow?" you ask immediately after.

"Meow?" Shelby asks.

"Yeah, bro." You laugh.

She laughs. "You mean 'now'?"

"Duh!"

"*Super Troopers!*"

"Hey," Connie blurts, "there's a couple music festivals down here that we could crash."

(Shelby turns to you, all of about four seconds, just you knowing, and tells you about how *Super Troopers* and *Superbad* are her favorite comedies. Those and especially anything with Leo in it.)

"Or why don't we chill downtown," Rob puts in his two cents.

"No," Shelby says, turning to the action. "Seems like we're always down there."

"Yeah, but downtown's kickass." Rob rolls down his window, air comes in.

Shelby just kind of pouts like whatever.

Connie goes, "The music down here, it's all sick."

"What are they playing?" you ask, still looking at Shelby as she looks out the window.

"Roots Shakedown," answers Connie.

You, Rob and Shelby look over at Connie, hyped at this piece of information.

"Are you serious?" Rob asks Connie for you three.

"Yeah. You guys didn't know?"

Things like "Oh my god" and "No way" and "I can't believe it" get said by you, Rob and Shelby.

Connie laughs. "You guys are silly."

Clock.

6:38 P.M.

"So how far are they?" you ask.

"They're actually in front of the courtyard in front of Rita's," Connie answers. "So yeah, we were just there."

"There wasn't anyone there." You laugh. "Damn, not much fans."

"It's a damn local band." Laughs.

"Oh."

"Turn around the car, please," Shelby says.

Connie passed the bridge and everything already, passing some island you went to when you were a youngin', but yeah, she turns back around on the dirtish road and she drives back around, weirdly. Y'all didn't know why she would've just recommended then pass the very thing she recommended completely, but that's beside the point.

You get there, passed the bridge. Before getting there, though, you see the island and remembered when one of your friends from Boy Scouts, on a camping trip there that your mom paid a couple hundred bucks for, did this one thing that killed you inside full of shame. It's weird, you were thinking about a time when you cried because you found this coconut on the ground while everyone was gathering a shit ton of them to eat. You found it and saw that it was absolutely perfect, like it couldn't get any better, all completely green and plump and perfect. You actually made it a pet, you called it "Pet." You didn't know any better, you were just a kid. Then a couple of your "friends" took it and ran with it and you chased after them, crying your eyes out, and after tossing it over you back and forth while you were all on the beach and you tried to get it from them, still balling your eyes and repeating "gimme gimme gimme I hate you gimme I hate you," they chucked it into the ocean. This is when you started to hate everyone, only at ten years of age, and even your mom told you it was a silly situation.

But anyway—beside the point—you and Connie and Shelby and Rob all park at some tree that's at the edge of the courtyard, with Connie not paying the parking meter there, and you all four walk out and, surprisingly, there's lots of people showing up.

"Wow," Shelby says, "maybe there was people here, but we didn't notice."

You walk around the car, hold Shelby's hand. She squeezes back and smirks.

Vaguely you feel like Connie is watching you two. She says, "Yeah, yeah, whatever, I hope it's good," but you're not looking at her to be sure of her damn body language.

Rob is kind of just walking, Connie looks like she's trying to hold his hand, and you and Shelby are looking like the cutest couple while you two walk together.

Middle of the courtyard. Awesome.

Roots Shakedown is almost finished with setting up their equipment and they are schedule to—

"Hey," you say, turning to Shelby, "when's it starting?"

"I don't know." She shrugs. "I guess maybe in a couple minutes?"

You say over to Connie, who finally just now held Rob's hand and they are walking off, about to do their own thing, "Hey, Con Con! When's this starting?"

She looks over her own shoulder, eyes batting, head tilted back, and she answers, "Seven!"

You don't even wanna look down at your watch.

Shelby, pulling you downward now, says, "Sit."

You do.

Shelby sits crisscross applesauce on the grass, not holding your hand. She has a smirk but looks at the stage.

You sit. You feel awkward. "I feel awkward," you say to Shelby.

"What?"

"Nevermind." You pause. "Hey, I left my car, I just realized."

Shelby says, "I thought you knew."

"Yeah, but . . . Forget it."

"Just enjoy the music, boo."

"Whatever." This drowning hatred washes over you, this fat sense that you hate every damn person on this earth. Uh . . .

6:58 P.M.

"Can I borrow him for a second?" Connie asks Shelby while standing in front of you, pointing maggot-ward. "Just for a second, hun."

Shelby rolls her eyes. "Sure." Then she whispers into your ear, "Be back soon before the show," then kisses you on the cheek.

You get up. You wipe the grass off your ass. The band is ready, up on stage.

Connie says to you, "Follow me."

"Okay." You say it like that one video game Odd World on the old Playstation 1, you think; Connie says okay, too.

She pulls your hand, leading you over to the bathrooms that show tiles with sea creatures painted in turquoise and bright green and pink for shells with some kind of sparkly glitter, and you both are suddenly shimmying against this little space between the bathrooms and the, you realize, moveable outdoor stage.

Connie looks up and around, curiously, wonderingly, and she smirks that coast-is-clear smirk, and though you are completely not down to be around her right now, she wildly looks at you. . . . Oh lord, and you knew it was somehow coming.

Shirt grab, pick up slightly, thrown against the wall, pinned, lips coming coming coming, and then—smooch smooch—she kisses you.

"Wow," she says after. "There's your make out you wanted."

You are actually kind of feeling sick.

"So, what'd you think of me?" Her eyebrow flicks.

"I have a girlfriend," you sigh.

"Who? Shelby?"

"Kinda, yeah."

"What's she got that I don't?"

"Nothing. I just said to make out with you earlier just to say it, really." You shrug. "I'm not that attracted to you."

Her eyes go big. "Wow. . . . Asshole." She wipes her lips with her sleeve. "What an asshole." Shakes head. She shoves you, pissed-faced, and you hit the wall, *bang!*

You see her walking off, so you say, "Wait."

She turns around. "What?"

You hesitate.

"*What?*" she repeats.

You say, "Lets, um, talk."

She turns around, walks closer. "You kind of just rejected me, dude," she says. "Not cool."

"I know," you sigh, harder than the first time. "I just . . . I just, I don't know, feel crappy."

"Well," Conner starts, "you should—"

"Hello! hello! hello, people!" an announcer says, cutting Connie off because of how loud, how much clearer, he is.

"Oh shit," she says after. "Okay, lets go—I'm not trippin' over this, I just thought you were cute. Lets go back 'n' chill."

You go back out into the courtyard; her like a boss, and you all kind of weirded out.

7:09 P.M.

Wow. Band's late, you're thinking.

You and Connie sit back down in the regular places: her with Rob, you with Shelby. And Shelby leans on you, head on shoulder, and she says, while holding the top of your hand in your lap while you both sit crisscross applesauce, "What did *she* want?"

"Lets just watch the show," you sigh.

Roots Shakedown plays effortlessly, awesomely, crazily, but they're a chill reggae band so it's kinda strange that you feel that way; maybe it's because this is your first concert. Always lots of firsts today.

There's very hot chicks, ages between eighteen and possibly thirty, but regardless, all still hot, and they are at the stage's edge's wall, clawing at the edge's corner, screaming, yelling all the band members' names, chanting them sometimes, shaking their asses while they do all this, and suddenly, angrily, you feel an overwhelming rage of jealously for these guys, so you pout, and though you do, Shelby asks you, after seeing you do it when she looks up from your kinda sorta chiny chin chin, "You okay?" Okay, it's not pouting that you're doing, but pretty damn close to a bullshit kind of face.

"You chill." You glance at her. "Lets watch the show."

She shrugs. "Okay, babe." She squeezes your hand tighter with affection.

Watch check.

7:14 P.M.

Now, you're trying not to concentrate on the fact that Roots Shakedown started playing without an awesome announcement or anything, they just started playing their guitar, drum and bass. The lead singer is vaguely a homie that you know. All the girls call him "totally dreamy." You kind of hate him because he actually is in fact dreamy—no homo—and you slightly wish you were him as he sings about mister mister president and respecting the youth and blah blah blah, all catchy as fork, and although Shelby, the hottest girl there, is all up against you and totally "vibin' out," as she puts it, you still feel the jealousy toward him, because you wish you had all the women in the world because they all look so great and desirable and nice and awesome with their big tits and big asses and lipstick and dressy dresses and cutesy curves and sweet things they say and the love they give and the love they receive back from the world; but even then you're jealous of them too. This is mostly so-called lame to other people, that you have this much want in the world. Some would call this "needy." Maybe it's the fact that you want to have money and nice clothes and fancy cars, just so you can distinguish your value in life. But regardless you feel like everyone is a F-ing savage that is looking for that one opportunity to better themselves and never others. Or maybe it's only you because you have been told that you are a fairly selfish person. Only once has this idea upset you, the idea of being selfish, but then it quickly subsided and was replaced with acceptance. Most would say that this acceptance is looked down upon because, honestly, who in the world would want to accept not only defeat but their acceptance of their own selfishness? You think it's like accepting Satan in your life, pretty much, but you digress.

For the passed four songs, which there's only five songs on the whole Roots Shakedown EP, Shelby has been kinda sorta dancing and waving her shoulders back and forth, so you finally ask her, on the starting of the fifth song, "You're a dancer, aren't you?" She just smiles looking up, then she looks back down and keeps shifting her shoulders into you as you both sit on the grass, dancing to the tunes. You just roll your eyes and grin at how cute she is. Then she swiftly looks back up and sticks her tongue out at you and you go, "Shelby!" "What?" she says back. You both laugh. Finally the song is done after everything.

Check.

7:54 P.M.

The singer, the one you're jealous of, announces that he thanks everyone for being there and Jah is number one and how grateful he is to be living.

Oh, piss *off!* you think. But you appreciate the music entirely, you are just a screwtard.

"That was awesome," Shelby says, clapping, then, turning to you, "Wasn't it?"

"Yeah." You start to stand up.

Shelby stands up faster, then pulls on your arm and lifts you.

You wipe the grass off your pants. "Thanks, Shelly."

She goes, "Only my grandmother calls me that," then she laughs.

People are all getting up and leaving, and you guess it's probably because the next person or band out is not as good as Roots.

Connie and Rob come up to you and Shelby, and Connie says, "Party time?"

You nod, but Shelby asks, "Isn't it too early?"

"It's dark already," Connie answers. "We could just drink if nobody's there."

"Oh okay." Shelby kind of makes a *whatever* face.

You all four start walking toward Connie's car and you ask Connie, "Hey, later could you drive me downtown after the party to take me to my car?"

Shelby intervenes. "Yeah, and me too."

"Okay, sure," Connie answers you both.

You all go to your doors that you were at originally; Rob in passenger's; Connie, naturally, in driver's; you in the back left side; and Shelby, the best thing ever, in the back right side, next to you. And Connie says, "Look at my hood, near the wiper blades. I got a parking ticket," and then she laughs and starts her car.

7:59 P.M.

Rob is asking, "Hey, beers?" to everyone, and then everyone in the car, aside from you, answers with, "Yeah, yeah, sure, sure" and then he pulls out a bunch of beer that Connie bought that's on the floorboard on his side. He leans forward, rips it open, passes out gold. When he gives you the forth one, though, you put your hand out shaking it away, saying to him, "Nah, nah, I'm okay," and Shelby goes, "No you're not," and she takes the can from Rob and sets it in your lap. Rob turns back around like whatever whatever. Shelby whispers, leaning close to your ear, "Come on, it's your last day. I want you to have a good time." You feel like total shit, but you say anyway, "Okay, whatever," then pop open the beer. You think that maybe Shelby knows it's not really your last day and maybe she's just kidding and going along with you, with it, the lil' beezy that she is.

You sip the beer. Wow. You can't even remember the last time you had one. The only time that comes to mind is when you turned twenty-one a couple months ago, a time when you were finding out that life really isn't that important because turning twenty-one equals you striving for a life ahead of you and trying to get the ball rolling . . . but only that, you realized, happens to people that have something promising going on in their lives. So you sit there, drinking this damn beer, the hops-infested, fermented potion that should drain all your sorrows away, and you wince at it, because it reminds you of the twenty-first birthday you had and how you, alone, got so drunk at an Applebee's that you were literally thrown out because you kept on talking to everyone and spraying out all your problems and making everyone "uncomfortable." So now this idea of drinking is the furthest thing you want to be going on, but you drink anyway because Shelby says so.

You look at her, then you look out the window. You're wondering why in the world you even liked her in the first place. Yes, you thought she was attractive, whatever, but a lot of people say that it's not what's on the outside, it's what's on the inside. But you tend to think differently than everyone else. You think that a woman's value is solely based on the fact of her looks, that her opinion and smarts are the furthest thing away from being relevant, that her "being down for you" has nothing to do with the attraction you feel for her, so, with this in mind, you tend to not only be scared to approach women for the simple fact that they can reject you but also because the courtship phase seems like a drag. If you ever fell in love with a chick, you think, you would be forfeiting your heart to her, which cannot happen. A woman can mess with your heart and use it and abuse it and mend it to whatever the heck they want. You have this feeling that all women are untrustworthy and impossible to love because they all want this power over you, especially the ones that in the first place you thought were absolutely gorgeous, usually the ones with looks that are as up to pare with models and actors such as Scarlet Johansson, Emma Watson, Emma Roberts, Carmen Electra, whatever; it doesn't really matter as long as there's wide hips, little waist, big jugs, perfect ass, plump lips, crisp eyes, long lashes, perfectly plucked eyebrows, and maybe a great smile involved, if you even end up seeing all that bull. . . .

Next thing you know, your beer can is empty. You just chugged it all because, screw it, you're tired. You ask the car, "Where's the gonja?" pretending to smile. Nobody answers you. Maybe you didn't actually say it. Maybe it was all in your head. You're never really too sure anymore.

"You guys ever heard of laser tag?" Rob asks the car. "You know . . . Fun Depot?"

Connie goes, "What kind of dumb question is *that?*"

"Yeah," Shelby says, agreeing. "If you live around here and haven't then you're missing out."

"I've never been," you say, timid, shy, whatever.

"Really?!" Shelby's eyes go big.

"Yeah." You're over it.

"Dude, we should go!"

"Nah," Connie says. "We gotta go to my place first. We're almost there."

"Shoot lasers," you say, "or get screwed-up?"

Connie briefly turns her head around and looks at you. "Screwed any day." She grins, turning back around and watching the road again.

Rob goes, "I was just sayin'. Right now it's free. Just got a text from my home-boy about it."

"Whatever," Shelby sighs.

Couple minutes more of driving, the yellow lines on the road zipping by as you look at them, your anger enrages. It fades, comes back, suppresses, comes back, leaves, then flows throughout your body and is replaced with depression. Nobody cares about anything but themselves, you think.

"Home, sweet home up ahead," Connie says.

8:21 P.M.

WELCOME HOME FUCKERS is stitched into Connie's welcome matt that you see right after you all had left her car and everyone closed their doors and you all passed some gigantic gate with an arch and then, passed a courtyard, came up her kinda sorta shared lawn, where you saw gnomes and Chia pets that probably weren't hers, and she mimics, during when you looked down at the matt, "Welcome home fuckers!"

You go inside and, immediately, Shelby holds your hand and stands all close by you, looking aimlessly, suspiciously, everywhere. Rob follows after you two. Connie leads the way.

"Not big," she says, "but home." She walks up to her dinning room table, which is the first thing you see when you walk in because of how much larger it is than the room's proportionate size, and she drops her car keys on it, *clang!*

This place smells like wood-chips.

"What's that smell?" Rob asks.

"My hamster and guinea pigs," Connie answers, striding into the living room, which is right ahead of the dining room.

Shelby is damn near suffocating your hand and is all super close by you. Maybe she's . . . scared?

You ask her.

"No," she answers, "just kind of . . . blah." Smile.

"I hear ya," you say, understanding.

From somewhere else in the house, as you and Shelby and Rob enter the living room, Connie asks, "Guys want coffee?" then, added after a pause, "I got the Keurig."

No, thanks, you all pretty much say.

"Suit yourself." Connie shrugs, putting the K cup in the little slot, shutting it after.

You look around and you see family photos everywhere, but they all look old and withered, like in an oval and framed old-fashion.

You ask Connie, "What are these pictures?"

She has her cup under the nozzle, the dispenser, it pouring, and she looks up and sighs, "I, um, collect things."

"Collect what?" Rob asks.

"I'm just a hipster, I guess." She laughs. "I collect old fash-ion photographs of people."

"That's . . ." you trail, "weird."

"Anywho." Connie picks up her cup and starts sipping, not adding cream or sugar, the psycho. "Lets just chill, yo."

Rob, grinning that oh-yeah grin, starts walking up to her as she sashays meekly into the living room.

Shelby still holds your hand. You follow, lead, to C and R.

You see them sit. Connie clicks on the TV with her remote. Rob says, "ESPN, yo!"

You roll your eyes and sit. Shelby snuggles up next to you.

"So," you blurt, clapping your hand together like a total ass, "what's up?" You want everyone to talk instead of just sitting there not doing shit.

Connie turns, saying, "Um, nothing . . . ?"

Rob. "Yeah, I don't know."

Shelby. "Good."

"Well, I wanna talk," you say.

"Then, um . . . talk," Connie says.

"Somethin' on your mind, brada man?" Rob asks. "Spill."

"Yeah, spill," Shelby adds.

"Uh," you hesitate. "Everything?"

Connie's all, "You know, forget it"—raises clicker—"lets talk." Turns TV off. Wowie.

"Nah, hun," Rob says, not being confident when saying hun? "Neeeeeed football."

Connie says that, nah, you have a point and you all should be talking.

"Okay, whatever," Rob says, more timid than you expect. "I guess I'm the bitch here."

Pause.

"So . . ." Shelby says, killin' the silence. "What do you"—she turns to you—"want to talk about?"

"I guess," you sigh, "I wanna talk about . . . Life."

"Oh god," Rob says. "Here we go . . ."

"No seriously, I wanna talk about Life."

"Okay . . ." Connie trails. "Um, what about it?"

You blink. "Uh, I don't know . . . the economy?"

Rob, again, is all, "Oh god—"

Shelby cuts him off. "Oh hush, Rob."

"Sorry, it's just . . ." He stops.

"It's just what?" Connie says. "We're all just stopping mid-sentence."

"I'm awkward for making you guys do all of this," you say. "Forget it. Lets just sit. I'm sorry I'm sorry."

"Nah," Shelby says, looking over at Connie.

Connie goes, "Agreed," then, to you, "The economy is, um, screwed, yo."

Shelby looks at you, but seems to say to Connie, "Why do you say that?" She squints.

"Because . . . I don't know, it's just . . . screwed."

"I feel you," Rob says. "I can't find a job anywhere."

"No, dude, Obama," you say.

"*Obama?*" Rob gets defensive. "Don't blame this on *him.*"

"Lets not," Shelby says, "talk about this, guys."

"Obama is mostly doing shit for himself," Connie says, sipping her coffee after.

You nod.

"What day it was?" Rob say, mocking an ignorant ghetto-fabulous.

You laugh at this. Connie goes, "Forever, trick."

You're thinking, damn, there was this cute, innocent barista blondie taking orders, smiling, being all nicey nice, and now there's this other part of her, not at work, and she is the most ruthless thing ever, saying "trick" or whatever.

Rob's all, "Okay, okay," slouching more into the sofa. "Um, how about . . ." He stops. "Uh, I got nothin'."

"You're not smart enough for this," Connie says to him, huffing a small laugh in the back of her throat after.

He goes, "Damn niggie." Laughs.

"What about," you start, "um . . . the differences between the insane and the sane."

Rob laughs again. "Stupid, yo."

"Lets hear him out," Connie says, squinting at Rob, then, "Seriously, lets hear him out."

"I think reality is subjective," Shelby comments.

"How so?" Connie's interested.

"It's all about who it is."

"Yeah, yeah, yeah," you say. "Yeah."

Shelby smiles her pearly whites at you.

"Bullshit," Rob says. "You're either alive or dead."

"Nigga," you say, though it's weird you said it, "what about the people who kill people? You think they had a choice? What if you love to kill people?"

Rob almost scowls. "Don't make it right."

"Yeah, what are you gettin' at?" Connie asks you, looking at you like you're nuts, vaguely.

You don't have to look at Shelby to know she's looking at you, too, like you're nuts.

Um, you've screwed up. "Nevermind. Forget it," you better say.

"No, pray tell," Shelby urges.

"Okay," you sigh, locking your fingers together in your lap, "firstly, lets say a person is born loving to kill people. And they do the act. To them, they don't know it's wrong, so why judge them?"

"Because it *is* wrong," Rob stresses.

"But it's their reality, the reality of it being right."

"So killing something is right?" Shelby asks.

You don't know how to explain this. "No. It's not right, but to *them* it is."

"What?" Shelby tints her head.

"Just"—you shake your head—"nevermind. Forget it, yo"—you, right after, turn to Connie—"can I have some coffee, yo?"

"You got issues," she says, shaking her head like a whore-bitch. "Issues, man, issues."

Your brain is freaking out. "Okay, guys! Seriously! Stop! This is just *my* opinion!"

Shelby touches your back, saying, "It's okay."

You look at her.

"Just keep going," Connie says.

"I don't know if you guys wanna know," Rob comments. "He's . . . uh, you know, a depressive."

"A"—Connie looks over at Rob, eyebrows all uppity up—"depressive?"

"Yeah."

"I get that way sometimes too." Connie shrugs. "It's okay—don't feel bad, _____." How does she know your name?

"Yeah," you say, leaning forward, chin in hands, elbows on knees, "I just feel like the world is so judging of people, that's all."

Shelby asks, "How?" She's all rubbing your back.

"Like, for example, commercials. All they show is just good-looking people, that's it—nothing else. Who cares about what we should look like."

"But that's . . ." Connie starts, coughs. "Uh, excuse me, woo. This coffee caught a knot in my throat." She coughs again. "Um, yeah, that's advertisement, yo, just sayin'."

"I know," you inform the bitch. "But imagine those ass-wipes in the newsroom or studio, saying, 'Hey, model, I want you to go get prettied up and then I want you to go in front of a camera and promote a product, regardless if you like it or not, and I want you to smile and make everything think it's cool and it's what you need to buy."

"You mean every*body*, babe," Shelby corrects flirtatiously.

"Oh hush," you spit out.

"Gee," Shelby says. "Jus' sayin', gah-*lee*." Eyes big, looking down, all surprised and wowed, at her side.

But, man, you're just trying to give them awesome information; things you care about in the world. You're just trying to help, trying to convey a bullshit message. . . .

"I'm just trying to help," you say.

"So am I," Shelby says.

"So basically you hate Capitalism, right?" Connie asks, taking a sip, the whole rim of the cup wrapped around her chin and lips. How is it not spilling?

"No, it's not like that, I just, um, I don't know," you say. "Nevermind. Forget it, yo."

Connie. Tilt head. "You seem sad, old chap." Smile. Awesome. Wow.

You're noticing right now the actions of others and the simple things they do because of reactions and things they were taught their entire life.

You. "Just sayin'."

Shelby. Stops touching you. "I'm just scared of your mind."

Rob. "He'll get out of it."

Connie. Turn to him. "No. This is different. I feel like he's"—looks at you—"a philosopher."

You. "I sometimes think that I'm a god in my own created world."

Rob. "You've said this before to me."

You. "I have?"

Rob. "Yeah, duh."

Connie. "Say more cool stuff," she tells you.

"Oh, um . . ."

Pause.

You say, finally, "I think I'm suicidal."

Room goes silent.

"No, seriously, I think I am. Don't feel sorry for me. I just see things different."

Same time. Shelby: "Because you're sick, babe." Connie: "You're suicidal, hun?"

You look at Shelby, saying, "Hate to break it to you, but I've been lying."

"Huh?" She squints.

"Yeah."

Rob. "Oh god."

Connie. "You want to *kill* yourself?"

You. "Yeah, today is the day I planned to do it. . . . Or technically tomorrow . . ."

Connie. "I call bullshit."

You. "Yeah, foreal."

Connie. "You seem so confident, though." Realizes, makes a sad-ish face, kinda high pitch voice. "Oh wow, this sucks. I don't want you to die. You're so cool, yo."

You're thinking about a sign that reads I HATE ALL OF YOU PEOPLE and this makes you feel sad because, um, who else in the world would think that? . . . Watch check, bro.

8:45 P.M.

"You shouldn't feel that way," Shelby says to you after.

Watch check again and—

Shelby, just then, has her hand over your watch, around your wrist, blocking it, probably just because, you know . . . whatever. "You listening?" Shelby asks you softly.

"Yeah." You are. "I am, I swear."

Shelby's all, "I hope you know that you shouldn't feel this way, babe."

"Yeah," Connie agrees. "We all really want you to live. Right, Rob?"

"Yeah." He shrugs. "I've told him earlier about our little bet."

"Bet?" Shelby asks.

"Yeah. He said that he has twenty-four hours to live. He's gonna do all the shit he wants to do before he dies."

"But where's the bet part?" Connie asks.

"I bet him that if he spent the day with me, the handsome devil that I"—flicks eyebrows up, down—"am, then afterward he would feel better and wanna reconsider his life."

Shelby looks at you.

"But what if he still doesn't?" Connie asks. "I mean, we should call cops."

You say, "Yeah, already been done before. A friend of mine, not Rob, told on me one, uh, night when I was losing it and, poof, everyone was scared of me and taking me to the hospital and blah, blah, blah, whatever."

This surpasses Connie in a way that almost feels like she doesn't believe shit like this actually happens. "What?! You got taken *away?!*"

Shelby, also in the same amount of shock, comes in like, "Yeah?" and this almost makes you feel weird that this a common trend.

"Whatever, yo," Rob puts in his two cents.

Nevermind. (Two to one.)

"Um, yeah," you say, "a cop came in and took me away—it's whatever."

"So badass!" Connie says, eyes big, all hyped.

"This is nuts," Shelby says. "I'm dating a guy who got arrested, pretty much."

"No," you say, without saying that they are all ignorant screwtards that you wouldn't mind just getting rid of altogether. "What's the time, guys?" you ask, knowing it already. "Wanna get outta here already."

"It's, uh," Connie says, "nine-fifty."

You don't believe it. . . . "No it's not."

"Yeah it is." She hands you her phone. "Look, hun."

You do and, wowser-bowser dot com, she's right!

"You mean this whole time . . ." you start to say. "This, uh, whole damn time"—you look at Rob surprisingly, disgustingly—"I've been behind over an hour?"

"Yup," he says, almost laughing. "Whatever time the time was before your twelve o'clock was also involved into your little scheme, *bingo!*"

You're trying to remember what you were doing for that hour, split-secondly, and, rather fast-like, a snippet of memories washes over your mind, like the fact that you woke up this morning and tossed and turned in your bed and looked at the ceiling with your hands behind your head and you thought that you were a crazy asshole just for even trying to consider going through with the whole "killing yourself" swareé that you think is going to solve all your pointless, meaningless problems on a permanent scale.

"Wow," you say. "Just wow. I never win, yo." One . . . hour . . . behind.

You spend about exactly fifty-six seconds trying to figure out how to change the time on your silly wrist watch, but then you also wonder how is it that your phone also was an hour behind too, and also, how long it's been like this. But while you figure this out, Shelby sits there, still next to you, looking at you, through you, in a severe daze you can't comprehend, and Connie and Rob are bitching and moaning about Connie changing her clothes, even though they were just the clothes under her Starbucks uniform, but Rob *insists* she keeps them, because it's a party and she is going to get "messy," as he puts it. *Zingo!*

9:53-ISH P.M.

Cooing all over you is actual God, not you, and he's all like, Hey, get your act together, yo, and though this makes you depressed, like everything else in the world does, Connie and Rob and Shelby get all ready and get up and you're the last one to leave the front door of Connie's house and Connie reminds you, turning around, "Hey, lock the door for me, will ya?" and you do by twisting the inside lock and shutting the door, following all of them after to Connie's car. You get in. Everyone . . . is . . . silent. Weird. Just weird.

"What's up?" you ask. "Why's everyone not talking?"

They still don't say anything. Maybe because they feel . . . uncomfortable? You don't know.

While Connie drives up some road you've never been, lurches passed a cop, buzzes on passed a semi, you think about how you told this one chick, Terri, that she could never, ever become a super-model because she totally isn't the ideal "it" girl that those agents, those scouts, those designers, those producers, whatever, look for in a striving model, though it was probably not true and you were—no, *still*—not an expert by *any* means;

you just wanted to give shitty advice to her gorgeous little self. She cried. You ruined her dream, you asshole, probably everyone thinks, thought.

Past-tense isn't your forté, all quite literally, even as you stare outside your window, you noob.

9:59 P.M.

Connie, Shelby, you, Rob, y'all are just crusin', mindin' bizz-nat. Shelby is talking to you about this one time she got so drunk at this one party that she ran across the house naked. Rob says he did that, too, once, but tops it by saying that after that he pissed on some model in Miami before. Connie tops it all off by saying she shit on a mattress. You all look at her like, What? You've never been to much parties to give a cool story, so you sit there, silent, but they all still ask you, Yo, what is your party story, bro? Eh, nothing, you seem to say to them, but they don't believe it. You guess you don't either. Whatever. Rock on. Connie is driving all fast as a blazing-on-fire circus monkey in a rodeo show, whatever that shit is, and she finally gets to the house party that she has built up this whole F-ing time. Out front, there's a bunch of black folk just chillin' like villains, smoking probably either weed or cigarettes—you're not too sure. Connie coughs out, "*Ah!* we're, uh! here, sorry, my throat . . ." and she turns her car off: key out of ignition. This is kind of the remix to ignition, hot and freshly out the kitchen, you think for some reason. F-in' poser. Shelby gets out of the car, walks around, holds your hand as you get out. Rob slings his arm over Connie's shoulder. You . . . are . . . all . . . Gs!

10:04 P.M.

Hey is all people never say around here. You all four pass the black dudes and, confirming that, yes, they are in fact smoking weed, the low-lifes, they don't even say a hello or hi or hey or piss off, they just stand and stare at you all, which is like saying F you, kinda sorta. . . .Yeah, so, the more inside, the more disrespect. Creepy crawlies all around the place. Trash already on the front lawn, cans and cig butts and possibly a used condom. Connie is all hyped, talking about how "screwed-up" she's gonna get. You think there ought to be about eighty-something kids there or whatever. You can already hear bass from a sound system bumping the ground beneath your feet. Shelby is still holding your hand. You both follow Rob and Connie as they pass the front door, the one full of low-lifes, and you reach a wooden gate that leads to a backyard. Rob asks if you could take his phone because he knows he will get screwed-up and he reminds you that the last party he went to he lost his phone and all that jazz and he doesn't want that to happen again. You take it and pocket it. Walking. The gate has an old-school latch. It's a crappy hinge that squeaks and pokes out and you havta wiggle the shit out of it. "Damn!" Connie blurts, "screw this door!" You shrug? *Whack!* it finally budges for her. Back to cool-guy style, you all four walk in. People are against the walls. Cig smoke everywhere; brume spiraling in front of an outside motion-sensitive light, cloudy. Eyes halfway open. Look up. See you four. Scold. Shrug. Back to own bizz-nat. About ninety or a hundred-something people out here in the backyard. This feels like that one movie *Project X* but casual and nobody's that hyped on it. There's five pong tables out here, two of which are not set up and are leaning against the back fence. Bunch of jock-asses are all playing, having red hoodies on, probably being from FAU but you can't be too sure. There's lawn chairs swarmed every-where, though, and you really wanna sit but—Oh shit, you lost Connie and Rob! "Where did Connie and Rob go?" Shelby asks you. "They were just around a secon' ago." You just shake your head, answering with an "I don't know." "Lets go mingle," Shelby says, tugging you. "Come on!" The music is loud, obnox-ious, playing some Drake song. Probably from his album *Take Care,* but you wouldn't ever admit that you do in fact like Drake and know all his songs by heart to these people. No way, José. Shelby is all moving around her shoulders and pulling you along. You see a girl you know. She waves and says your name excitedly. You wave back like whatever; you remember her be-ing a cunt to you before in some math class in middle school. Grudges, yo. Anyway—Oh, and just FYI, you're not a racist. But yeah, you go passed some whore-bitch named . . . Eh, screw it, you don't really know. Shelby knows her, says hi. The girl doesn't say it back. The girl's yellow shirt says, in red marker-felt type font, RAVE IS KING. . . . Great. And she has glow-sticks looped over her middle and ring fingers and under her index and pinky, both hands, moving them excitedly, almost too much so, and she is flourishing them in cyclones and circles in front of some kids that sit in lawn chairs and their mouths are gapped wide open, movie Grudge-style, eyes wide and watery. And they are almost ever so slightly moving their heads to all the motions she makes, you kinda notice. And then there's a couple people coming up, circling around her, as if this just now started, and this rave chick is all super into it all, moving her eyes and head and shoulders and hips around like a conductor for an orchestra, all insane 'n' shit, and the song changes immediately when you see all this happen. You know what it is. It's by Deadmau5, called "Raise Your Weapon." Everyone is all serious, not at all making fun of this ordeal. Shelby tells you to come on, we're gonna be late! even though you think, Late for what? So you get pulled on by her and leave this sight. Next thing, around the house a bit, a BBQ is grilling, unattended, and the hotdogs on it are smoking out and burnt to a charcoal-black crisp. Nobody cares. The fire is not too big. In fact, it's just the coals that are rosey-red. "Ember" is what you think it's called. Above, there's kids on the roof, sitting at its edge, smoking joints, obviously, and they dangle their legs and you see this but then, ouch, dirt hits your eyes from one of the F-er's shoes, the bottom part. They don't notice this bullshit happening to you. Not even Shelby. She drags you along. You shimmy between a long line of people that are waiting to fill their solo cups from the, um, four F-ing kegs there is. One Bud Light, one Corona, another Bud Light, and a Dos Equis one. But nobody goes to the Dos Equis one because it's most popular and already tapped. You see Connie and Rob off near the backyard's corner fences between all these people in line. They are talking to some jock who you knew from high school. He's changed a bit. He once actually gave you a swirly as a joke to mimic to his friends about all the corniness those '80s movies do to show what high school's like. You just so happened to ran into the bathroom while he was explaining the idea and he, swoop, grabbed you by the shirt and dug your head into the toilet, flushing one, two, three times, laughing while he did it; his friends too. He looks good right now from afar at this party. Better than you do at least. He probably doesn't remember you. Nobody really remembers anyone they messed with in high school. Shelby doesn't spot Connie. Probably because she doesn't care. She says to you, close to your ear, shouting because how loud, how booming, the music is, "Lets go inside! Get some drinkies, boo!" You think she said "boo," but you can't be too sure. You say to her, "Sure," not shouting, and she nods, probably saw your lips lip it. She keeps holding your hand and you go passed a bunch of people. It's kinda sorta dark, you think. There's a door, a screen door, and it's centered and connected to the inside. Front house, go around, gate, go around, screen door, go around, another gate, go passed that, back to the front lawn. The house is kinda big, but this is pretty much it, plus the big-ass backyard. Anywho, you go into the screen door with Shelby. A dude comes out at the exact same time you guys go in. He cops a feel of Shelby's tit. She screams, "What the hell, asshole?!" He just laughs and runs away. "Ugh!" Shelby blurts. "ASSHOLE!" This did piss you off but you're pretty passive about it, considering Shelby probably has, like, double-F titties, the MILF that she is. You go into the house. Immediately you smell vomit. It's right to the side on the floor in the corner of the room, yuck! "Eww!" Shelby says. "What kinda party is this?!" You were just thinking the same exact thing. Anyway, you keep going. You see a table and around the room are paintings. One of which is super colorful with a guy smoking but it's not realistic at all, none the least, and though you think it looks Picasso-y, it's nothing you'd ever consider buying at a goddamn show if this person did one. Shelby pulls you, leading the way. Each person you shimmy passed, you think the words: she . . . has . . . no . . . idea . . . where . . . she . . . is . . . going. You finally get to some kitchen. Or is it . . . a game room? You don't know. There's a bar and a mini fridge and a big-screen TV, so maybe it's not the kitchen, but who knows, right? You don't judge. Shit's baller. You say, "Shit's baller," and Shelby goes, "Huh, boo?" You just say nevermind. On top of the mini fridge is a punch bowl full of what you're assuming is Hawaiian Punch, because there's two empty bottles of it on top of an overflowing trashcan on the right side next to the mini fridge, on the floor. Two empty Bacardi bottles are next to the punch bowl and you think, Oh lordy. There's an unopened bag full of stacked blue solo cups also next to the punch bowl. Shelby rips the bag open and grabs out two, handing you one of them. There's a ladle in front of the punch bowl, sticky and dripping, and she scoops out a heaping amount of this F-ed-up punch and pours it into your cup carefully. She smiles then she fills her cup in the same way too. People are all around but nobody is around this fridge. You notice everyone has blue cups in hand so you guess they all got their fix. Shelby goes, "You are in for a killer night." You answer with, "Yeah, totes." She smiles. She taps your cup with hers, then downs the shit. She sighs, ahhhh, after. "Damn!" she blurts, looking at the cup, squinting. "This shit is crazy." She points at it, looks at you. "Try it. So *strong!*" You look down into your cup and because it's kinda dark inside the room, the liquid looks like a dark, dark black, like coffee. You make a piss-face, an *eww* face, but take a deep breath and slowly lift the cup up to your lips. You stop, though. Shelby's all, "Just do it, chicken." You look at your watch.

10:22 P.M.

How in the world massive amounts of people are here, you don't know. House is too small, seems like. You decided to say, "Look over there" to Shelby. She turns. You pour the shitty-filled drink on the ground casually, without her knowing. A girl is screaming "Yeah!" at the top of her lungs. Shelby turns back around and comments about it, saying, "What a lame-ass bitch," though you're thinking Shelby did the same exact thing in your car earlier in the day.

Above you, red and yellow and blue balloons are helium-filled and floated to the top. A string dangles. You jump up and grab it. Shelby is looking out at the people, grinning, having fun. You pull the balloon down, letting go of your drink Shelby gave you, dropping it to the floor. Try to hand the balloon over. Shelby goes, "Aww! You're so sweet," but then loses interest and says, "Lets see what *they're* doing!" Yanks you, leaves her balloon.

Move to the kitchen. There's an island, shelves for snacks, bunches of cupboards, dish washer, sink, the average mumbo-jumbo. People are penguin-walking to get to the bottles of tequila and vodka. Empty ones are set aside to show how "cool" they are with the amount they drank, you guess.

There's two dudes hanging out by the counter. Shelby walks up to them and asks, "Could you pour me a cup, cowboy?" and he responds with, "Sure, cowgirl," grinnin'.

To them, you ask, "What's this party for, man?" trying to be friendly. They say they have no F-ing clue, kid. Get lost. . . . Rock on, bro!

They pour her a drink. You walk over to a cupboard and grab a glass, come back after. One of the dudes is talking to Shelby now. You walk up, the dude talking to Shelby turns his back to you, blocking. The dude's friend taps your shoulder. He goes, "Hey, lets talk." He puts his arm over your shoulder, walks you away. "Listen," he says, "beat it." He shoves you, walks on off.

You see the guy that was talking to Shelby sling his arm over her shoulder, all index finger pointing chest with cup in hand, laughing, having fun; her laughing and having fun too. . . . And, wow, you're just entirely over it.

Forget Shelby, you think. She's just like all the other girls you've ever had "a thing" with. How you can't entertain them and keep their love. How they always go for the bigger and better. How you feel like you're always the chaser and they never give you the time of day, going off with jocks and punk rockers and movie stars and handsome male models. . . . Maybe you're not good enough to love. Maybe you're not special.

You make yourself a drink. Jack Daniel's bottle and a 2-liter Coke. Mix mix, bro. Jack 'n' Coke inside a red solo cup. You're thinking, I fill you up. Lets have a partaaay! Awesome. Not really, though.

You turn around, bump into the chick that was yelling "Yeah!" at the top of her F-ing lungs, and she turns to you, smiles, yells, "Yeah!" Go figure.

You shimmy between the gaps of primates looking for a good time. Everyone has either really nice clothes or something you wear to the beach. Such lame-Os.

Before going out the front door, you decide you're gonna have some fun, so you grab a couple red balloons and run. They slant backward and tap and catch at the top of the front door's frame.

Outside, you jump up in the air and feel a sudden rush of happiness, so you let go of the balloons. You stare up at the sky. Little red dots going smaller, smaller, gone, into a black endless void.

"Hey," Rob's voice says. "Been lookin' for ya."

You turn, look at him.

"Where's Shelby, bro?" he asks you, sipping a beer, Bud Light, the blue kind, the one that changes color when it's cold enough.

"She is . . . I don't know." You look over and passed him and see everyone all running around like the children they are.

"So . . ." Rob hesitates. "Um, Connie and I are no longer."

You squint. "Why?"

"Don't know. She was a punk bitch."

This makes you laugh.

Rob grins. "What?! It's true."

"She forced a kiss on me at the Roots concert," you admit cautiously, for fear that maybe Rob will get offended or mad or some pussy shit.

"Bullshit, bro." He is totally not buying it, as you can tell, whatever.

"Yeah man," you say. "Foreal. She took me back and just . . . kissed me."

"That's messed-up. . . . Tell more," Rob urges.

"Eh, forget'm." You start walking.

Rob is following. "Whatchu drinkin', bro?" he asks, coming up next to you.

"Jack Coke Jack Coke Jack Coke Jack Coke," you joke, saying this a million miles per hour, "trick."

Rob is laughing. "Where ya goin'?"

"I wanna play beer pong," you answer. "Duh."

"Oh." Because you both come up to the tables just then, waiting up in line, minding bizz-nat, crusin', stuntin', whatever,

Rob bellows, because of how intense, how deep, his buzz probably is, "We got winner!" and the dudes there just grin and say back, louder, "Hell yeah, son, we gottchu!" and the line is like, What the hell, man? because they probably have been waiting forever, but Rob has this confidence, this drive, to say F it and YOLO.

Back and forth the jocks go. Before they talk about who won the super-bowl in something like the '90s, they cover the house rules for you and Rob briefly. Say the Dolphins suck and are so washed out they will never have a come-back. One of the jocks says that that's bullshit, because he is in fact a Dolphins fan, straight outta Miami, and screw you, bro, they will come back. *Bam!* Dolphin's fan jock sinks into a cup.

Dolphin fan says, "Diamond," referring to the house rules, because there were only five cups left before he just made the shot.

One then two then one, that's the rows the loser jock just makes. He says, "Whatever."

Rob puts in his two cents by saying that the Seahawks are gonna slay every single person in the NFL, considering their defense is "unstoppable" and "ruthless."

"Yeah right," Dolphin's fan jock says. Sinks another shot. Balls back. Gets another turn.

You stand there, silent, and look at your watch, not even thinking about anything at all, anything worth shit, while sipping your—

10:43 P.M.

Nevermind that. You're just trying to play a game of Beer Pong. Dolphin jock misses the first ball but then Rob asks if he can have a celebrity shot. Dolphin shrugs, saying, "Whatever." Holds it, the pong ball, out.

Rob takes the ball from him. Rob stands center. One eye closed, other open. Taps the ball on the edge of the table. One foot back. Eyes down the cups. Puts elbow back, swoops the ball over the air, over the beers, rainbow-style, and it swoops and dives straight into the red solo cup.

"Damn," Dolphin's fan jock comments to nobody in particular, then turns, asking Rob, "What's your name, bro?"

"Greg," Rob lies. "And yours?"

Dolphin holds fist out. They dap. "My name's Greg too," not just a Dolphin's fan jock anymore says. "That's weird, bro!"

You have a hunch Rob knows him and he lied and said Greg to Greg because he knows Greg is probably an F-ing tool and he wants to make fun of him. "Yeah, I know, bro."

"Can we be teams?" Greg asks Fake Greg.

"Sure," says fake Greg, then, suddenly realizing, "Oh shit, never mind." Turns to you. "This is my teammate."

Real Greg looks at you. "Sup. . . . S'your name, bro?"

You say, "______." You think real Greg says "bro" too much.

"Cool, bro." Real Greg turns, continues playing.

Rob steps aside, coming up next to you. Says, "This guy went out with my sister in high school. He's a faggot. He's probably too drunk to remember me."

You knew Rob was gonna make fun of him, you just knew it.

Only two cups left for Greg. Other guy has five. He sinks one in one of his pong shots, but then misses on his second shot. Eh, whatever, he's probably thinking. Balls back to Greg.

He smiles at other jock. "You're screwed, Freddy-boy."

"Oh piss off," Fred laughs.

Sink, sink, twice. Both shots made.

"Game over," Greg says.

Fred goes *pfft* and then walks off, like a punk. No hand-shaking or good sportsmanship goes on.

Greg turns to Rob, saying, "You're up."

The line of people are now making a group with their backs to the game, conversing about, you think, college classes.

" 'Kay," Rob says.

Greg goes, "But um, we been playin' one-on-one rounds. There's a comp goin' on."

"So." Rob squints. "Your point?"

"Whatever." Greg turns to the line, saying, "Need a part-ner!"

A chick comes up, saying, "Oh man oh man!" hyped.

She stands next him. She has little tits but a perfect ass. Greg slaps it, smiling. She doesn't seem to mind. He turns to you as you just stand there in your same spot. He says to you, "Are you gonna play or just stand there like a duck?"

"Oh, um, yeah, I'll play." You walk up next to Rob. Rob whispers to you, "We got this."

You and Rob are putting the cups in a triangle that points at Greg. Four, three, two, one is the rowing. Greg does his side faster because he's drunk. And because he probably does this every single night.

"Your go, or our go?" you ask.

"Ours!" the chick with fat ass, small tits, says.

"What's your name?" you ask her, almost in a mocking kind of way.

She doesn't notice. "Kayla."

"Cool beans." You put your hand out, as if to say, *Go, you stupid bitch. Your turn!*

Greg is chugging his beer from the last game he won. The beer, it's foaming down both sides of his chin. He goes *ahhhh* after. Slaps Kayla's ass again, batter up!

His one eye is open as he aims with drunken precision. Bloop-bloop. Throws.

It's going, going, going and . . . Doesn't make it. Oh shucks.

"We got this," Rob says to you. "These niggies are gettin' too drunk to play."

"I think the drunker, the better, yo," you figure.

"Yeah, but only for a couple rounds. Then after awhile it's just the drunker, the more screwed. *Ha!*" He laughs. "Let's watch."

Kayla's up. She looks overly serious. It's cute. She's wearing a shirt that says "With Dumbass" and it makes you laugh inside. She tap taps the edge of the pong table with the ball, with her pinchy fingers, and she has both eyes open and moves her full arm upward, missing the cup completely.

Rob says, "Elbows, bro."

She goes, "So what! I'm a girl. Bite me."

You and Rob laugh. She grins.

"Our turn," Rob says, sticking his tongue out after, to her. The bastard is so damn flirtatious is not even halar' 'lar', you think. Whatever. He says to you, "Go first."

You nod. "Okay." Batter up.

You're eying down the table and the triangle is straight in your sights. You launch that bitch in the air and, *swoop*, it goes in, solid.

"Damn, son," Greg comments. "Nice."

"Thanks," you say.

"My turn," Rob says.

"I'm bored," Kayla complains to Greg.

"Okay," he says, "me too," then, to you and Rob, "You guys wanna call it a game?"

Rob squints. "Um, what the actual fuck, man!"

"Sorry. I'm pretty hammered, bro," he says.

"Me too," Kayla says. "Been drinking so much shit in the line."

"You guys are pansies," Rob says. "Whatever. We didn't get to play, yo."

"You guys are pretty cool," Greg says. "You wanna do somethin' crazy?" He's walking around the table toward you and Rob. "You guys wanna do something nuts?"

You nod. Rob just says, "Uh . . . maybe?"

"Follow me," Greg says, waving toward himself. "Got something to show you guys." He steps forward, slings both his arms over you and Rob's shoulders.

Watch check, yo.

10:59 P.M.

Eleven o'clock not on the dot. Dang it! but no matter what you're never, ever going to be happy, you guess anyway.

"So, where are we going?" Rob asks Greg as Greg guides you and him to somewhere, anywhere. "And yeah, I need a beer."

Greg grins. "Go get you one, brother Greg." All three of you are now by the back porch light and under it on the ground, against the wall, is a cooler. Greg opens it up and, *splish-splash*, digs his hand through the ice and he pulls out some brewskis, hands them to you and Rob after, whatever.

You say, "Thanks."

Rob just cracks open his.

Greg asks you both, "Hey, you guys ever done fire mummies?"

"Fire mummies?" you ask. "Nah." Shake your head.

"They're awesome," Greg says, leaning back down to pull a beer of his own out.

"What is it?" Rob asks him, sipping his bullshit.

"It's pretty much"—Greg has his beer, standing up, now —"um . . ." He is looking at his beer, tries to crack it open. "What the hell, dude?" He is trying to lift up the lip and then, *pow*, it opens and foam is spraying out. "What the fuck!?" Greg blurts. "Who the hell shook it?!" Nobody answers him. "Whatever," he says, and sips his now half-full beer. "Anyway, fire mummies are, um, pretty much you get a bunch of toilet paper and you put a person in the shower—"

"I'm sorry, what?" Rob says, stopping Greg's explanation, alarmed and flabbergasted like how you are too. "Um, yeah, what the hell, yo?"

"Just listen, Greg," Greg says to Rob. "Okay, so you pretty much put a person in the shower and you wrap toilet paper around them a shit-ton of times. Then you get a lighter, a buncha lighters, and you have everyone light pieces of their toilet paper on them—so like on the arms, legs, chest; everywhere but the hair, of course. Then the person gets set on, um, fire"—he starts to laugh—"*ha-ha*, and then they freak out and it's, oh man, so fun, bro!"

"Sounds friggin' stupid," Rob says, squinting enthused.

"Yeah," you agree.

"I'm tellin' you guys, man," Greg starts, "you should do it —"

"Hey!" Kayla interrupts, coming from the F outta nowhere. "Bro! You gotta make a better freakin' party!"

Greg turns to her. "Um, you beezy, shut up."

"We're brother and sister by the way," she says to you and Rob.

"Didn't he slap your ass?" you ask.

She doesn't hear. "Don't you guys think this party is kinda lame?"

Rob looks at you and you look at him. Rob turns back to her, saying, "Um, yeah, um, kinda."

Greg seems irritated. "Sis, it's not your bizz-nat."

"Trick, it's *my* birthday!" she says.

Greg turns to you and Rob, thumb pointing at her like she's crazy, and he says, "Women . . ." He blows out, *pfft.*

"Oh shut up!" Kayla says.

Greg smirks and hugs her. She smiles, saying, "Stop it, bro, stop!" and he says after, "My lil' sis is eighteen!"

Rob whispers to you, close by, "Eighteen, huh?" You look at him, his eyebrows flick up and down. You roll your eyes, laughing. This guy . . .

"So ______," Greg says, "whatcha thinkin' with the idea we got?"

"What idea?" you ask.

"I heard you guys . . ." Kayla says, grin grinnin'. "Fire mummies, right?!"

"Yeah, nosey," Greg says to her.

"Lets do it!" She jumps up and down. "Yeah yeah yeah!"

"Yeah. Lets," Greg says.

Rob turns to you, gives the *You think it's cool?* look or signal.

You say, "Sure, yo," very monotone.

To all, Rob is like, "Only if ______ goes first!"

Kayla looks at you in this really obvious, seductive way, coming closer, and she says, "Oh yeah, baby," and then she slings her arms over your shoulders. "Lets gets you fired up!" How come girls like you? you think. And then you think, How drunk is she? You don't think anyone knows, really, and quite frankly, if they even care.

11:08 P.M.

Though it's better to go, to glide, to shimmy, through the booming, thumping crowds, a quivering sense of deviation from reality into psychosis rushes ceaselessly through your brain and this makes a bleak, almost comfortable perception, and the savage, ruthless animals, all wearing their pointless, meaningless threads, around here, you think, are so totally weird or whatever to want to gain some kind of dark possession toward acceptance, in the same way your psychosis just now rushed through your body, in the same vicious way you don't want to live anymore and you want to just leave, go home (whatever that place is), buy a switch blade along the way from some bum or thug, curl up into some lame cocoon in the corner of a dark room, and slice your arm from the hand first and then all the way down to your inner elbow and smiling that you're done, over, kaput, *zingo!* but tenfold over more than these people's bullshit.

Greg and Kayla, the lovely people who threw this party—who are leading the way—just have to say hi to everyone, because they know every single F-ing person, but then they stop and continue to lead you and Rob through the whole house, through the whole crowd, and then you all four eventually come up into the bathroom, but wowie zowie, dude, people are already in there, right there, in the porcelain Cave of Wonders. And guess what they're doing, go figure. . . . Fire mummies, yeah. Greg goes, voice cracking, "Holy! When is the next one up?" Someone, laughing so F-ing hard that their cheeks are red for some reason, says, "You can go now, bro!" but this makes Greg heated, blazed, red at the face with a blue vein popping from an adrenaline rush of rage that make you laugh to yourself in some cute way.

He says, "Everyone *out!*" People turn around, still laughing, saying, "Oh shit, it's Greg!" and then they all say "asshole" or "dickhead," jokingly, as they pass him and you and Rob and . . . You forgot her name. Oh yeah, Kayla, duh! They keep pouring out the doors and pat backs like they all are getting some childish inside joke. Greg just laughs. You really don't get how people can be so mean and know the name-calling is on joking terms, is on *laughing* terms. You think about a time you and a kid named TJ or something, both age nine, tried to spend the night over his house and you had some kind of weird gay encounter where you both humped your bum bums with clothes on, under covers and everything, and this makes you wince and cringe with such a screwed whatever-whatever embarrassment that make you instantly wanna . . . Watch check, you adorable little sunflower you. Because you can't wait for this lame-ass day to be over.

11:17 P.M.

Rob is all, "Um, this is friggin' stupid" and then he stops, turns, looks at the bathroom's mirror. He's eying himself, moving his curly black hair though his fingers, picks his teeth, sucks them, and then turns back around at you, Kayla, Greg, then, all lame, says "What?" to you guys; probably not being embarrassed like you are right now because he doesn't have stupid thoughts like you.

Greg is all laughing, but probably not because you all four looked at his actions as he turned around after checking himself out, whatever. Greg goes, "This party is wild" and then glances and walks over to the shower.

You walk over to it too. You look down. Wow. There's little black balls of soot and paper swimming in puddles of mud, of sludge. Up in the air above you, mixtures of smoke or mist or brume are spiraling, curving, everywhere, making the roof's paint bubble, decay, buckle inward. But probably it's taken a long while to make it that way. You instantly think the people who live in this house, meaning Greg and Kayla, are irresponsible, are crooked little sixteen-year-old twenty-something-year-olds.

From behind you, Kayla is looking over your shoulder, saying, "You're up."

Rob says, "This is nucking futs, yo."

Greg squints. "Isn't that from *Dickie Roberts?*" he asks Rob.

"Yup." Nod.

You step warily, disgustedly, into the shower, your feet crunching something like plasma or goo, something like black poop squishing probably between the ridges on the bottom of your red Converse you bought at a skateshop called Shred Shed.

"Now you," Greg says, motioning Rob briefly toward the shower.

Rob goes, "I wanna watch, yo, but thanks."

"Nah," says Kayla simply, her back to you all, not looking, arms already inside a pantry, grabbing rolls of, um . . . T.P.? You assume so!

"Ah, shit" is all Rob says, then he rolls his pant legs up to the knee and very cautiously steps on into the shower where you're at. You scoot over, giving him room, space, all that, whatever. "Ah shit ah shit," he repeats. "Dammit this feels weird!"

Greg laughs, saying, "It's usually dry, bro."

Out comes Kayla's self into the open. "Here I am! I'm back!" and she has two fat rolls of toilet paper, the Charmin Ultra kind. Maybe they're rich, you think, or have caring parents, or both.

"Okay, now we gotta mummify you guys," Greg says, taking a roll from Kayla's right hand. She has the other in her left, ready too.

You and Rob are standing there, defenseless? No. That's not the word you're thinking. You're thinkin' . . . unprepared? You don't know really.

At first, Greg, so excited on the inside that his outside is serious-looking, takes the roll's end off and rolls it one, two, three, four times around his wrist as he steps toward you and Rob. He takes off this wrapped wad and drops it to your feet. He kneels down at the end of the shower, rolling the roll up your ankle, then up to your knee, then higher, higher. He's at your waist.

You look over at Rob. Kayla is beating Greg in the rolling department, by the looks of her being at Rob's chest and Rob looks like a human snowman, how now white he is from how covered up he is, duh.

Greg is now at your face. Time, you know, is flying, soaring, wrapping itself in T.P. around bodies. Greg is wrapping the paper around your forehead, then around the back of your head, then over your nosey nose. Vaguely you see in your sights a half blur of white and Greg's face, smiling at what it has created.

"Oh yes," he says, nodding, looking up and down. "Hell to the motherfuck yes."

You look over to your right and see Rob looking at you too. He's all, "What the hell have we gotten ourselves into?" but he's shaking his head and you think he actually probably is hyped but masking it with purposeful composed maturity. You know his ways. . . . The ways of a person caring about, well, you know .

. .

From his back pocket, Greg gets out a Bic lighter, it being purple. Kayla talks about how purple is the rare color of Bic and she's jealous and wants to know where Greg got it. Greg doesn't pay much attention. He asks you and Rob, "Ready?" You consciously watch check.

11:30 P.M.

Saying "yeah" is all you can say on a last day to live, so you say yeah (go figure) and watch Rob say yeah too, by the looks of his single nod. Kayla is pulling out a lighter, like how Greg did, and they both excitedly step toward you and Rob as you both stand there like mummified dorks, no curtains to hide you both . . .

At first, Greg snaps the lighter and out presents a burst of flame. Then he pushes the tiny, tiny lever on the metal tip to the highest setting, making the flame shoot up about an inch more. He keeps it up with his thumb on the button. Leans toward your feet. He's still kneeled, mind you. At your ankles, he lights both sides. Takes a second but then lights up. You look over. Rob is lighting up, too, from Kayla's doing. Back to your feet. *Bang bang*. The flames are lapping upward!

Greg is lighting your chest. Side to side he moves the lighter and your chin is down, looking at this happening. A black hole opens, widens outward, and burns deep with fire. Suddenly your hands feet hot, then your legs, your chest, your face. Your everything is lit up. Smoke is kind of in your eyes.

Rob and you are jumping up and down, saying, "Oh my god oh my god oh my god OH MY GOD!" and Kayla and Greg are laughing.

You're jumping and flapping your arms like a bird. Stepping. Knees up and down a million miles-per-hour. Up down up down. Stomping. Oh my god, you are actually on fire. Flames are blaring. Your ears feel hot. You hear Rob laughing so hard, screaming, "Holy shit holy shit!!"

Greg's voice asks, while you notice you and Rob spinning in helpless, mindless, unsafe circles, on fire, "Tell me when!"

"Now now now now!" you and Rob are saying. "Holy shit holy shit, dude! Now! NOW!!"

You hear a squeak, a loud one, one that hurts your ears. The sound is obviously rust mixed with steel. You feel a rush of cold water explode from above you and trail down your body like a waterfall. Rob is next to you, pushing, needing this just as much as you do.

The fire is going out! Oh man!

You're getting soaked but the fire at your feet is not entirely out. Rob is stepping out of the shower, laughing, all saying, "Holy shit! That was awesome!"

You have a wide smile on your face, staying in the shower. You lean back and feel the wall stop you. You hold onto it, hands flat. Wow, you feel an adrenaline rush. That wasn't what you expected! You close your eyes.

Rob's voice says, "Get out, man. You're gettin' soaked." You feel him tug at your shirt. "Come."

You open your eyes and step out. Rob has his arm over your shoulder. You hear about how cool it was and other things that seem inaudible because of how shocked, how anxiety-fied, you are.

The door opens. You and Rob step out. You hear the shower-head squeak somewhere behind you. . . . Watch check.

It's broken. Probably from the water. You ask Rob, absently, "What, uh, time is it?" and he answers with

11:37 P.M.

"Why did we get outta there so fast, yo?" you ask Rob another question as he's pulling you out and into the party's living room bullshit.

"Because you looked like you were gonna faint or . . . something."

"Hey!" a male voice shouts.

You turn around over your shoulder; Rob too.

"Hey hey, wait!" Greg says, running toward you guys.

Rob is hyped. "Sup?!"

Greg's like, "Holy shit that was fun, yo! You guys wanna drink?"

You nod but nobody really sees; they usually never do, you think.

Rob says, "Hell yeah!"

"Come." That's Greg. He waves his hand and Rob follows him; you do too. Crap, though, you feel hella soaked. Your hair is dripping. Funny thing is, though, is that the people in the living room are just as soaked with sweat from probably hardcore dancing. You try not to notice this.

Finally passing all them, you and Rob and Greg get into the kitchen. Greg looks through the tall pantries. Nobody's in the kitchen, really, just in the living room, dancing. It's loud.

Greg is pulling out two fat handfuls of shot glasses and has to keep them all close to his chest to keep from dropping them. He puts them all on the kitchen counter. Rob is standing them all up. You're watching them work.

Greg is going through the fridge and is totally grabbing out a big, fat bottle of Jack Daniel's. Oh yeah. He puts it on the counter, near the shots. He grins.

Rob looks at you and says, "Oh yeah, niggie."

"Lets get to it." That's Greg. He twists the top off the Jack bottle and pours into all the shot glasses. Ten of them? You count. Yes, it really *is* ten.

The shots are poured. Greg pinches one of them, hands it to Rob. Rob hands it to you, pass pass. Then Greg pinches two in each of his hands and, again, hands one to Rob. Greg says, "Salute."

They toss their drinks back like nothing.

You follow; you always do. Toss back. *Ahhhh!* Wow. Strong!

"Another?" Greg asks you and Rob.

"Sure," Rob answers.

You nod, you guess.

Another pour sesh from Greg.

Another "Salute!"

Toss back.

"Another?"

"Hell yeah!"

Pour sesh. There's still the other seven.

You grab a bunch and one, toss, two, toss, three, toss, four, toss, five . . . You drank too many. You feel like shit. But hey, it's one helluva night, you guess.

"How did you do that many?" Greg asks, surprised.

"HEY!" Kayla's voice (of course) says. "Why did you guys start off without me?" She's pouting like a lil' bitch.

Greg's like, "Men's time."

"But *I'm* the birthday girl!" Still pouts. "Gimme that!" She steps forward and pours a line of Jack to each shot glass, in a row, the liquid spilling on the counters for every other one—but you guess, Who cares? Does your watch work? You look. It does.

11:47 P.M.

"Oh my god!" Kayla says. "I'm gonna get shwastey!" and she does every F-ing shot she poured out. Goddamn, she's a trooper! She belches and Greg tells her, "Jesus Christ, Kay!" and she tells him to piss off and that he's a pansy. Then she looks at you and asks, "Hey cutie, what's the time?" She grabs hold of your wrist and you both look at your watch. *Ugh.* Again, again, again. You hate this goddamn thing.

11:47 P.M.

"Almost Midnight," Kayla says, turning around toward Rob and Greg. Then she says, facing back around at you again, "Screw it" and grabs the back of your neck and pulls you toward her sweaty, alcohol-smelling face. Kiss kiss. *Boom!* You weren't ready for that. This startles you. What if God was one of us? you strangely, suddenly think.

Greg is laughing; so is Rob. Are they drunk already? Probably. But probably not. But probably they were the whole time.

Kayla stays holding you. She throws her head back and shouts, "Woo! I'm"—she throws a fist up in the air—"freaking wasted!"

You are pretty much disgusted by her. Though it's possible she is your type when depressed and thinking about women that are hot and that party their lives away, all you seem to think about, crave about, is Shelby. "Hey, Rob, where is she?" you ask. Around you, Kayla, the party, Greg, everything, are all making noises that roar with mindless excitement.

"Where's who?!" Rob shouts back at you, squinting, taking a sip of his bullshit shot. Weird.

"Shelby!" you answer. Your thoughts never compute with the outside world. It's like your brain moves two steps ahead of the world. That's actually a huge problem, but whatever.

Rob points outside, toward the window. "Saw her somewhere out there, I think!"

"But I was pretty much with you the whole time, dude!" you say, thinking he makes no sense.

"Bro, I saw her when we got in here! You were zoned the hell out!"

Remember, you both have to shout in order for your shit to get—

"Heard . . . that, Robby-boy." That's you. You start to hold your head. "Wow." The floor looks spiraling and looping with the likes of its terrazzo's random spots, intertwining with the puddles of beer and cig butts and . . . "The room is spinning," you say. "*Crap!*" You bobber your head slightly up. Nobody's listening. . . . Good. Now get the heck on. Somewhere Greg says to you, obviously without needing an answer or explanation, "I thought your friend's name was Greg."

Ignoring this because you're screwed-up, you turn and kind of shift your body just to walk straight. You're trying to get through people. Hey, watch it! Hey, what the hell?! Yo, bro! Eww, dude! Move it! *Bleh!* Walking out of that nightmare in the living room, the front door is finally at your face but it almost seems like fiction. Being skunk drunk is horrid.

Immediately you fall over frontward but catch yourself with the door's frame. You hear Rob's voice yelling some kinda shit somewhere, maybe-probably explaining his whole lie to Greg on his name he said.

You are looking up at the sky with your arms out and you spin. Your legs tangle into a knot, kind of. Ha-ha. The sky is dark and beautiful. You can't see any stars because the motion-sensitive porch light is vaguely blinding you.

Everyone and their mother is here. There's beer cans all over the floor. If you say "beer can" out loud, it sounds like you're saying "bacon" with a Jamaican accent. Fun fact into your noggin'.

You are starting to walk and step and penguin-move over to somewhere you don't even know.

Oh look, it's Shel Shel.

"Hi!" you shout. You are seeing the back of her head. She turns around but, um, it's not really her.

"What the heck, bro!" some dude says, with long black hair and a physique like a hottie, a girl hottie, mind you.

Your eyes go wide. "Well, excuuuse *me!*" Talk to the hand, broski, walk away.

A girl, you notice, is talking about how she wants to go to the army, the marines, whatever, because they have good benefits and, though she never wanted to before, she's saying she needs those benefits for her family of five that she ultimately wants with the husband she doesn't have yet. A drunk kid comments that she's F-ing crazy because settling down sounds like a nightmare to him, even though he's obviously a college kid, going off to have a dope job, dope life, dope *lifestyle*, all that, and your anger rises then plummets from being punch drunk.

You're stumbling and mumbling something under your breath and your lips quiver and drool slimes out of your maw like a dog. You stumble into a group of people circling around an invisible campfire, looking down at it, talking. You place your hand on some guy's shoulder.

"I's is dee bestest everrrrrr!" you slur.

You here something like, what is this kid doing? but pay no mind to it because they laugh after saying it. You start to slur a bit more and hear a girl talking about a vacation up in Hollywood that she wants to do so she can go up there and see how it, like, really is, and hopefully muster up the courage to move there and become famous.

"Bullshet," you say. And then you hear a "who asked you?" but whatever, you start to hold your stomach, aching like a cow on acid, and you lean forward, hand still on some guy's shoulder, and your lip is quivering, warping inward, doing uncontrollable things, and then you hear a long *wahhhhhhhh-woooooooo* sound coming from your bowels deeply as a knife slicing through a bitch's leg. "I'm gonna barf," you admit, almost whispering because of how much it hurts, how much is pierces into you, then, *bleeeehhhhhhhhhhh!* you hurl a fat load of chunked vomit right on top of the Hollywood girl's probably expensive high-heels.

She screams, "What the hell, asshole!" and the guy with a shoulder holding a barfing guy's hand literally pushes you then tugs your shirt and spins you around and gets in your face, raising a fist, and you put your hands up, scared.

"Hey!" a familiar female voice says, howls— sorry. And she scoots that dainty arm of hers between you and this brute-forced trick with a fist aimed directly at your pea-brain head. "Back up!" the dainty arm girl says.

The brute guy is shaking his head and puts his fist down and lets go of your shirt. "You're lucky," he F-in' says.

Your eyes are blurry and your head hurts and pounds, piercing into your eyes, causing hysteria and a migraine.

"Hey," the dainty arm girl says, putting—duh!—the dainty arm over your possibly speckle-vomited shoulders. "______, you gotta be more careful." You can't believe she knows your name, so you look over at her. . . . It's Shelby. "Missed me?" she asks super sexily. "I think so, my big man."

"Can we sit?" you ask. "My head hurts."

"Figured that." She rolls her eyes, guiding you over to the lawn chairs that are empty and scattered everywhere, toppled or upright, whatever the case. "You get yourself into some serious shit, man."

You look for the time. Okay, that watch is bullshit. You look down and you walk with Shelby and see a chick on her phone, texting, leaning into it, eyes on the screen, its shine lighting her face blue. At the top of her screen it reads

12:13 A.M.

Over there—

Shelby grabs a white lawn chair and still has her arm over your shoulder and she lifts the chair up and sets it up straight for you and you sit in it being entirely cozy, slumping everything into its seemingly deep socket of a bum-rest.

Strangely there's really less people in this little cement slab area. It's just chairs. Everyone is all scattered over the backyard; nobody wants to sit, the drunktards.

Shelby scoots next to you, very close, with her white lawn chair; she is grabbing the front part between her legs and tip-toeing.

"Hey," she says to you, "everythin' okay?"

"No." You bury your face into your hands. "I'm so friggin' drunk, man." You feel bad, too, for doing it, the drinking.

"It's okay, boo." Shelby is really concerned, probably. She is patting your back. "Listen," she says. "I'm sorry I ditched you. I didn't even like that guy. He just came onto me and made me laugh at stupid shit. I really like you, not him. I should've known what they were doing. He got weird and really only wanted to take me home with him."

"Really?" you ask. "Fuh."

"Yeah," she keeps going. "And um . . . then I looked all over for you and I couldn't find you."

"I was just inside." You lazily point toward the house with your thumb.

"Yeah but it . . . I don't know. I couldn't, um, find you."

"I don't think you were looking hard enough."

"I was!"

"No."

"Ah, come on!" Shelby urges, kinda, to nothing in particular.

"Do you even like me?" you ask. "I mean, at all?"

"I'm sorry, _____, I screwed-up!" She pouts.

"Yeah, you did, big time. You ditched me and forgot about me."

"You're drunk. It wasn't like that. I looked for you."

You shoo her away. "Whatever. For the birds."

"You're drunk *and* mean," she jokes.

You look up. "I don't know. I'm just sad."

"Aw. Just sit 'n' chill 'n' cool it. Relax. Not a lot is"—she puts her hand on your back—"going on."

"A lot is. I want nothing to do with this life," you say.

"Dude," she blurts, "life's not *that* insane."

"Yes it is . . ."

"No it's not."

"I can't find happiness anywhere."

"Because you don't allow it to happen. You just sit back and live to die. Nothing in your life is worth shit at that point."

"Uh . . ."

"Look. I'm tired of being nice. I like you . . . a lot, and I've said this before to you. But you don't seem to care or expect it to be true. You just don't believe, and you just say 'screw it' too much."

"Because you're gonna lose interest like all the others."

"What makes you think that, _____?"

"Because I'm actually a screw-up, Shelby. I am. I'm unpleasant and no good. Nobody likes me."

"No, not true. You are the one that doesn't like you. That's the guy you should fix."

"How can I possibly even like myself? Myself is lame as hell and screws up!"

"Shhh . . . Voice down!"

"Sorry, Shel. My head hurts."

Now, lets get real: the really real real reason you're so up-tight about Shelby is because, through all the bullshit you're going through, the partying, the love, the friends, the being-on-fire, the fact that you want to kill yourself in just about half a day's hours, you think Shelby should at least be more supportive of you and your crappy endeavors; you know, because it's the *least* she can do. . . . As you think this bull, you're saying nothing.

Shelby breaks the silence. "So, uh, your head hurts where?" This makes you think she's stupid, but then you look into her eyes, into her connotation, and you see that she's being suggestive, you hope, bet on. "I mean, you know, if, um, you want it to hurt," she says, flicking those perfectly plucked eyebrows of hers up and down like a black girl's twerking ass.

"Are you trying to hit on me right now?" you ask. "That's hot." Smile. "Kidding."

"No!" She seems serious. "I'm just talkin' whatever . . ." and she is looking up at the sky, at the birds she can't see, and this, again, makes you friggin' . . . FRICK! Don't mention it, Narrator, you're thinking. Gosh. "Hey," Shel says to you, "you know, I should confess something."

"What?" You think this outta be terrific . . . not.

"I used to like girls."

"Really?" Wow. That actually *was* terrific.

"Yeah," she says, her voice lowering. "Long time ago."

"How long?" You say this but you know it's stupid and probably insulting to ask.

"Um, like, four months ago."

What? You bury your face into your hands again, and this totally makes you uncomfortable. The info she's giving, not the burying, silly.

"_____?"

"Yeah?"

"I dated this girl named Kayla."

Oh.

"And she was really great to me for a long time."

Oh, *oh!*

"And she was special to me and never did me wrong, but I ended it with her because she started partying a lot with her brother."

"I'm *sorry?*" you say, having to stop her because this can't be F-ing real. Meaning to you this can't all be one big F-ing coinky-dink. "Um, you dated a girl named Kayla?" Shelby nods. "And you broke up with her because she partied a lot?" Mhm, she says. "What does this girl look like?" you ask, more trying to not put two and two together.

"Well, um, she yells alot." Check. "She's hot." Check. "Can't hold her beer for nothin'. Ha!" Double-check. "And she's a total pyro." What . . . the . . . helly hell.

"So, uh, how did you guys break up?" you ask, voice cracking. You cough. "Eh-*hem,* sorry."

"It's cool. Well . . . we were at my job and she started to drink too much at the hookah bar, even though there's no beer allowed at ours. Then she smoked, like, a hundred *dollars* worth of hookah. She cheated with this girl or whatever. It's just a long story."

Too long, you think. But as Shelby talks more about her (how Shelby doesn't know where she is or where she had lived; how she used to act; how her wardrobe was; et cetera), anxiety, in a roaring way, flashes an endless plethora of memory polaroids that stack one by one on top of each other. One of them is an old picture of your mom and good ol' dad riding around in the car, happy, arms up, and they want to live life. And though it comes up, a sharpie etches its way over and writes GIVE ME BACK TO HER, which makes no sense and you have no idea what the symbolism is. Another one shows a hamster named Wizard your parents bought you when you were two years old. And another is a photo that probably your older brother took when you drank too much at his birthday and he totally took it to show your embarrassed self in the morning, and then you had to clean up the vomit on his lawn. You don't remember a goddamn thing about your life.

"______?" Shelby says, and then, rubbing your back with one hand, holding your hand with her other, "You okay, sugar?"

"Yeah, I'm fine," you say, over it entirely. You push her off you gently. "I just feel sick."

Shelby briefly asks you, "Hey, have you seen my purse, ______? by any chance?" but you ignore it.

And just then, out from the depths of a greater hell, a sluggish, partying trio, by the names of Kayla, Greg, and Rob, come up all together behind you, and Kayla, probably not noticing

Shelby, says to you, "Hey! Where you been?! We've been—" She stops, notices Shelby most definitely. "Oh, it's *you*." You look over at this devil-like Kayla and there's quite a mean mug written across her face.

You start to stand the hell up and ask Rob what the time is. He says don't worry about it, but you urge, press, for it. He finally says it and it's

12:29 A.M.

Kayla says, "What's up?" Shelby, over it-like, says, "Sup?" Kayla asks, "Why are you here?" Shelby says she has no idea why; she just came with you, and she points at you. Kayla says she thought she told her to beat it, sister, and that she never wants to, blah blah blah, ever see her ever again. Shelby, sarcastically grinning, says, "With pleasure, sista" and this makes you think of her as some kind of movie or something you saw when you were five. Rob is saying, "Hey hey hey! Stop!" and he's serious as a heart attack. Greg is saying to shut up, Rob, because he's still kinda pissed at him for lying about his name.

You start to walk away from this situation of assholes, but Shelby stops you by saying, "Where the hell are *you* going?"

"Somewhere else," you say.

And Kayla goes, "I kissed him. I hope you're not dating . . ." and this makes you F-ing hate Kayla because she forced that kissed onto you and she knows it! Or wait, was it Connie?

Oh my god, and guess what the next thing happens. . . . After these lames start fighting and bitching a moaning about their past affairs, a drunken Connie comes stumbling into Rob, saying, "Hey sexy. What's—" and then she stops and looks at Greg. "Holy shit," she says under her breath, and you think you're the only one that heard it.

Rob is totally oblivious. "Hey Con Con!" says him. "Where you been? Missed ya!" and then he tries to give her smooches. Something stops him.

An arm around a neck. "What the heck, bro!" That's Greg. He looks at Connie, still with an arm around Rob. "Who is this kid? You screwin' him?!"

Connie just shakes her head, swallowing a "got caught" knot in her throat.

Under his spit and gagging, Rob says, "Why are you, *ugh*, friggin', *ugh*, choking meeee?"

Again, Greg says to Connie, "Who is this kid?"

"He's just some guy that made out with me and I didn't want him to," she lies. Then turns to you. "And him too."

Shelby looks at you in a way that says "you gotta be frickin' kiddin' me." But Greg has a look at both you and Rob that's like, "I'm straight up gonna gut these niggies."

"Wait! No. Hell no," you blurt to Shelby, but also to everyone. "That girl's a liar!" Not much use.

Greg shoves Rob into the grass. He comes at you, raises his fist, elbow up, face clenched along with a stretched square of gritting teeth, and slams and clobbers you into the ground, *slam! wham! bam! bunk!* and Shelby starts screaming, noooooooooo!

Up above you the world seems smaller and the cosmos spider-web of stars glitter their constellations amongst each other, crowning King Gregory the Third, pissed and angry and jealous-fied, and he . . . spits at you. "Bitch!"

Your eyes feel swollen, and a piercing, stretched feeling spreads across your face, making a garnished, swollen-purple bubble of a bruise on top of red and yellow scaly skin. The ringing in your ear turns to psychosis and you hear Rob step behind Greg, yelling, "What the hell, bro?!" And then he socks the living shit out of the guy, Gregory, but little Gregory doesn't drop, not even the slightest, because football has obviously prepared him enough to take a hit or tackle.

"Little" Greg spins his upper body and hooks a fist straight into Rob's stomach, *pow!*

Rob is holding it, choking out a "Ugh!"

You start to sit up and see Kayla tugging on beautiful Shelby's hair. They are fighting and it's about to be a, what? a girl fight! And you totally are indifferent because a random thought of them two swimming naked in the middle of the Bermuda Triangle and then disappearing comes at you in multiple, unknown waves.

These are some of the things you hear: a face smacking; a bone crunch; a shirt rip; a heart beat; a person yelling "yes"; a girl screaming; a jock hurling a whistling football in the air and into his partner's arms; a clanging bottle; a laughing crowd; a girl getting screwed by a black guy in some car down the street; a shooting star soaring; Shelby saying to snap out of it. . . . You're drunk.

Shelby screams, both mad and sad, "Why would you kiss her and not tell me, ______?!"

Boy, oh boy. You just think about poor ol' Shelby, poor, sweet Shelby, balling her runny mascara-ed eyes that drip drop down her cheeks and bleed and inkblot black smudges of pain and falsified belief.

"She made me!" you say.

You hear Rob grunting and smacking Greg's head dully (because of how drunk, how over it, he is) into a sleeper-hold, with arms, both him and Greg's, flaring. The arm of Rob sling-shots out and darts back into Greg's spine, again and again, re-peating, and Greg, though probably faking it, grunts, too, but more louder than Rob. Greg spins and grabs onto Rob's shirt and pile-drives him into the cement, back-first, and then slides him into the brick wall, headfirst. "Ouch" is an understatement.

Connie is just standing there enjoyin' herself. You remem-ber a television program that promoted safe sex. But that seems irrelevant now, at first, but then turns into something more philosophical. Like the fact that people are savage to the ones they love and adultery is completely natural but is considered taboo, so they made a program to instill a thought of abstinence (or attempt to) into your fresh, love-free, adolescent noggin'. But the TV listeners become lost in their reality of "it's my life and I can do whatever I want with it."

Random fact: it takes an average person twenty full hours of a "good time," which includes texting, dating, movie-watching, et cetera, before going into sexual intercourse.

It takes an average of twenty seconds for a person to go psycho. It takes twenty more seconds to be closer to your death. It takes twenty or no seconds to decide to kill yourself.

"I hate you, _____! I hope you die!" Shelby screams, but you don't think she means it; she's just upset, is all. "I mean it!"

You start to fully get up and stumble. Off in the air is the sounds of . . . sirens? No. It's just the air. Honk honk. You are up and start to run, and though it feels like you're going fast, in reality you're probably not. You bump into people and push them aside and automatically you become that one kid at that one party that people saw who got so hammered he rudely pushed away everyone just because he was drunk and probably was being a total D-bag. Behind you is more fighting and yelling and grunting, and you have a feeling of hatred.

You stop, just right outside the gate you stepped into at the beginning of the party. You think of it like a machine. You go in sober and then you go out drunk. But you stop before getting out and start to lean against the tall wooden fence that laps around this party. Its horizontal lines bend and sway. Your eyes feel like they are crossing. Your head pounds, swells, thumps, and your stomach, flabby now from high-calorie drinking, is making guttural noises. "Gonna barf," you whisper. "Again—" and, *blehhhhhhhhhh!* it comes out like a geyser, straight onto the front of your shirt and down at your right pant leg. Fat chunks, somehow. You don't know. It's brown and gooey and smells like the tart smell of dirty baby.

Echoing, you hear someone yell, "COPS!" and everyone in the party is running behind you, but you instantly feel a rush of sobriety engulf your body and you, fast as a mother-frick, pull open the wooden gate and bolt the F outta there, in first place toward a possible . . . freedom? Maybe you were psychic about the cop sirens. You see blue and red lights flashing against the asphalt and the grass and a tree out front. Flashlights are up. Two dots are waving inharmoniously back and forth, trying to search for out-of-hand drinking and loud-as-hell adult/partiers. One of the lights spot you, and the being behind it says, "Hey!" You start to run like you've never ran before, down the street.

Just then, a beaten-up Rob is behind you, tugging your shoulder, running with you. "Dude!" he says, "lets freaking RUN!" and this makes you think, Duh, no shit, Sherlock! Then, noticing your threads, Rob says, "Oh my god, bro!" He's laughing. "You yacked all over yourself!" For the life of you, you try to hold back a punch to his face, but realize Greg did all that for you. So, um, yeah, you say nothing to this asshole. He goes on, though, like, "That bitch, Connie, is such a F-ing liar! I can't believe that! She cheated on him but blamed it on us! Sick, bro! Just sick! Whooped the kid's ass, though." You're thinking, Yeah right, yo . . . This guy.

You both are still sprinting down the sidewalk, passed hell rows of cars, but then cut into a neighbor's front lawn and stop.

"You think we're okay here?" you ask Rob.

"Yeah, we're fine."

You sigh, go into your pocket, take Rob's phone out, though he doesn't get it, and you read and then realize it's

12:51 A.M.

"You're really gonna do this in eleven hours, bro?" Rob asks you. "It's sad."

"Yeah. I am." You're feeling sick, wobbling.

Rob is concerned. "You looked haggard."

"I am."

You see a light post and a bird and you think of them as sightseers gazing out the tour bus.

"Yo!" Rob says, snapping fingers in front of your eyes. "Snap out of it. We gotta go—"

Whoop whoop! a cop car, lights flashing, sirens, cutting Rob off. Stop. Cop opens door, stands out, and yells, "Hey, you two! STOP!" Did they bring backup? Holy smokes.

You and Rob look at each other and split.

You feel sober again and you sprint behind the house and there's no fence. You vaguely look behind you and see the cop chasing after Rob, not you, thank God—because Rob plays soccer and he is more athletic than you and has won awards 'n' shit, like trophies.

You're in the backyard and see some bushes and run for it but then a Rottweiler barks and chases after you but you get to the bushes and the dog yanks back because he's attached by a chain in the ground and vaguely you see a sign on the back sliding-glass door window read BEWARE OF DOG.

You're passed the bushes and see Flagler looming up ahead of you and you kinda think you have no idea where you are, even though you know it's just Lake Worth area, but that couldn't be more vague. You're in a neighborhood and there's a lake in front you, and around the lake are endless houses that tower with a garnish of, um, luxurious blah blah blah. F you. You hate people with money.

All the houses are nice but as you swiftly creep passed them like a zombified cyclops with one eye open from the piercing, shining, shimmering, splendid street lights above you that pulse rays of light with every movement of your one eyeball, you feel more in Hell than you have ever been. The walkway stones crumble. Your sightless eyes see no stars, no bright dots that have a life, a better one—one that is prosperous and full of uncanny amounts of happiness, you hope for, crave for, live for, breathe for, die for. . . .

You're circling around the lake but then see a big, open entrance with a gate that reads THE ESTATES and this makes you roll your eyes because of how lame, how gay, how stupid, it is, saying something fancy like that, knowing damn well the people here are lower middle class and trying to hustle and bustle. . . . Lame.

Anyway, you pass the entrance and then cut a right and you realize there's a bridge and the train station is there, but you know it doesn't run at this hour and also you have no money.

Crap! But whatevs, you're just alone and walking. Oh look, a bum sitting on a curb, drunk. That's nice.

You walk and walk and walk and then pass the bridge and see downtown Lake Worth, where Roots Shakedown played earlier, you notice the night is more livelier than the day, which is odd, but nonetheless is giving you a sense of complete relaxation, or probably that's just the highly sedative effects of the amount of alcohol you have consumed.

You pass by hella stores and lights, ones that are signs and blink and pulse and gleam exotic colors, like highlighter-green or orange or blue, but anyway, the stores around are like random shits, listed in coordination: galleries that aren't open, pawn shops, grocery stores, clubs (one with a, *duh*, neon sign that reads PROPAGANDA), and so, so much F-ing more. But it all seems blurred, even as people pass you like animals passing a dead carcass that has been eaten up and the only thing left is its bones and a memory.

You realize you've walked a mile now and it all doesn't matter; it doesn't feel like any real time has passed. You don't even care about the time anymore. Everything is all a blur now, tonight, as you lurk into drunken-town and cut into sober-town. . . . Oh, look. You see another bridge. It's one you saw as a kid when you were in boy scouts and, um . . . Wait. You already been told this story and thought about it earlier. Screw it. Turn.

You're on Flagler. You're actually worried about the time so you watch check. But . . . it's broken and not going to be on any-time soon, not in your lifetime anyway. So you undo it and pinch it and toss it over the wall that has the intracoastal way down below it and the watch makes a *splat* and *dunk* noise and it slaps against the water and this makes you, though completely unresolved, relieved. You see the moon and it's full and round, and it's so bright that it gives you a headache.

You pull out your phone but, crap, it's dead, you now remember. No telling who has tried to call or text you. Cut off from communication. Cut off from everyone. This moment is not much different from your entire life. But that's neither here nor there. You chuck it, too, like your watch in the same way, but in your other pocket is Rob's phone. It's dead too. You keep it. It's not your property to throw, but you think in the mean time it's considered "your phone" until you give it back. You know it's about five more miles of walking down Flagler just to get to City Place and then to the parking garage where your car is. You put "your" phone back into your pocket and except that you don't know the time. . . .

?

It's a fat, long, straight-away tiled, cobble-stoned walkway, and it's literally five miles of pure cold, silent air, you probably think. You see a small speck of a pink building, the Trinity hotel, very far up ahead that seems to be close to your destination, but you are seriously penguin-walking like a drunken idiot and realize that it's gonna take you all night to get to that building, probably. You do have time, though, to think about things for once today. You never got a break to actually put together a series of uncontrollable, undeniable, unheard-of reasons to die in this little life you're in. The biggest one is this lack of connection with others that although comes in splits of waves, darkens between other's perspectives and your outlook. This idea that we are human and that we are just simpletons looking to grab our next meal, though endless, but create a point system called money to better regulate our motive of operation. The word "fuck" is a fowl word but only because people have made it so. If you say it then people wince and call you an asshole. It's a simple sound but it causes electrical systems in the human brain to decide to confront this so-called disrespectful person. Your whole life revolves around this face because you apply it and notice it too much in your waking life. All of life is a marry-go-round system that although others excel at, you fall deep, deep down into some unknown depression, anxiety, and psychosis, which doctors have insisted before is normal, is completely natural and normal, and nothing is wrong with you, Mr. ____. Then you left the doctor's office and realized there is no real people anymore. Just jobs. There's only animals seeking a meaningless, aimless purpose in life. It's not about right and wrong anymore; it's about survival; about who is the one that's gonna be on top. . . . And then there's that moment when you realize all your life the problem was you, when you realize that everyone may have been right, when you realize that everything you think you know is meaningless, when you realize that all of this shit in the world is just carved out of fabricated wood, when you realize that this is nothing to be stopped, when you realize help cost all of your money, when you realize there aren't any resources left, when you realize that everyone's smile makes you sick to your stomach, when you realize how jealous you are, when you realize that you are lower than low, when you realize that you have so much but so little, when you realize that everything is crashing down on you and it's all an optical illusion, when you realize that everything is in your head, when you realize that the laughs are all fake, when you realize that you're depressed, when you realize that all of everything suffers, when you realize you can't stop it, when you realize that you wish you could help, when you realize that you wish you felt good for once, when you realize that you care too much for so little, when you realize you're just like every little piece of decaying matter aimlessly floating down every stream and everything is a constant war to try and survive for this one thing call happiness, when you realize it's funny. And more things you think about: Every time you see hot chicks you always think of the behind-the-scenes, where she's texted ten times a day "hey, what's up" and has two missed calls from numbers whom she doesn't know, or the guys she gives her number to to make them leave her alone, or the guys that say the average "you're beautiful," "you're awesome," "we should meet up sometime," blah blah blah crap. And you keep thinking about all of this and for once when these girls cross you and get the chance to speak to you, you tell them, No, I'm busy, no, you're not my type, hands off the merchandise, no, go away; can't you find someone more you're type? and so on and so forth, then they frolic toward you, go figure. Wow. The world is weird. The idea of freedom in the wealth/poverty sense of the word, makes you cringe and baffles you beyond levels of sanity. If you're poor, you must depend on things and services to guide you into the right direction, like government loans, et cetera, but you always have this idea in the back of your mind that makes you want more. This is where it all gets tricky. If you get above a certain mark, the services are not granted to you any longer, so therefore you struggle to make the leap. Humans make the leap, fine, dandy, but sometimes when you reach a certain level, you gain a level of comfort and plateau out into a plane that makes you no longer have the drive anymore, which may or may not lead you into being poor again. Your question: if the rich are rich and the poor are poor, and we all are the same type of humans, why is it that the money is passed around in certain areas at certain times and more "hotter" places? Seems like the rich can network better than the poor. Usually the rich hang with other rich and they share great advice and great investment opportunities. This is where the saying "rich get richer, poor get poorer" comes from. The poor people hang at places where other poor people are, because they share the common class and are not monetarily privileged enough to attend the places the rich would be at to further expand their own personal class. So everyone stays the same in their own class they are born into. You may be asking yourself, _______, why are you even thinking all this borin' shit? You'll tell yourself you visited Austin, Texas, to see a friend of yours this one time, back when you were in high school and your parents had money to visit the family that was there. You saw a taste of a life that you wanted. But how do you get it? The art world there, the women, the happiness, the freedom, all of it showing in abundance. . . . Now, not saying this place is for everyone, but it got you thinking about goals. Goals are great and lovely, but you somewhat feel as though this idea of the "American Dream" is more or less in the fictional spectrum of America. The possibility of getting out of the funk inside the middle class or lower class is probably as nonexistent as Santa Claus or the Easter Bunny. This idea that "if you do this, you get this" seems much more broader in nature. The risk involved with it all is virtually endless. You took a step back from your life and had to reevaluate your situation. Firstly, you're a full-time worker, early twenties, male, white, and I have a huge passion in Fine Arts, more into the digital side, with tablets 'n' shit. Fine, dandy. But that demographic is more common than you'd think. If you truly want to be successful with art, first you must define the success you want. Do you want millions? Do you want fame? Do you want blah blah blah? If you take a step back, you could say you're successful in art, like winning awards 'n' shit. But why is it that you feel unsuccessful? Lets say you wanted to be as big as the greats, like Basquiat, Warhol, et cetera: what would you have to do to achieve that? Ah-ha! Now you see a taste of your world. You want something that becomes fictional. Something that becomes luck. This is where your world falls to pieces and you have this looming, grueling depression seeping everywhere around you, around the people involved in it, and you're a physical repellant to your peers. . . . Now lets look at another thing: reaching your goal. If reaching that goal means networking, the perfect place is college, unless you kill yourself today. However, the risk involved is so exponentially high that it almost seems more worth it to go at it alone. However, you personally, you could care less about the education part of it (what would you be paying for then?). You can learn anything from a book. College, however, grants you something you can't get from a book: Experience, a degree, proof. It sets you up and prepares you for success. . . . Well great! That's cool! Okay, so where do you start? This is where your enthusiasm falls: you lived in Florida and received a highschool diploma with a 2.2 GPA. You have no connections, no money, no helping finances from family (because they have their own plates to handle, which is perfectly normal and average and you want no hand-outs from them), and a full-time jobbie, trying to pay for bills, on the verge of a mental breakdown from this adulthood. On top of that, you resent education. You always test the knowledge of everyone because you find it hard to believe that someone could know more than the person who showed them their knowledge. You're very much an autodidact, a self-taught person. You resent learning from others because you would much rather seek your knowledge "out in the wilderness," so to speak. So, this in mind, if you go to college, you have to work full-time, have to maintain a lifestyle, a social life, et cetera, and you have to do this for years. But then you think about where you're at and its location. It's not Austin, TX, the place where you dream to go, so it depresses you because you're not there. Then you look at the huge percentage of your peers with degrees who have received the same amount of success (and in some cases less success) than you. These are the factors in your life to make the decision. You do not want to take to risk what you will regret later: spend all your time, your money, your everything, into this bullshit, just so you can turn out to be the same person you were when you started and gain absolutely nothing close to the level of success you want, which is already impossible to reach as it is. . . . This is your life. This is where you stand. You feel for the people of this world who have to go through this and face it. We are all trying to survive and be humans, trying to put food in our mouths. What screws us over is this "lavish" lifestyle we think we want, all trying to be kings and queens. You hate it because it's not even really something you can work for. You highly believe that your level of success is directly related to the living world around you that you are given each and every step you take in your life. So disappear it, you think. A car comes, you crash, you fix your face, you change, you do this, you do that, et cetera. The list goes on and on and on. . . . Ugh, you hate all of this jargon you're spraying out into the world. Bottom line: your "success" (whatever that could be) is determined by four things. One: your situation. Two: your drive and level of wanting. Three: your resources (and in most cases this means the level of money you have to fund your passions). Four: talent (self-explanatory). You hate how this system works because you have yet to see real results of something that didn't have all these factors included. And if you do, for example, find it, like the idea of the thousands of people who go to L.A. to try and become big-time actors, you just think about the rare winners and how great their lives are, and then you weep over the thousands of losers who didn't, couldn't, make it. Then you just see yourself as one of them, further making you depressed and ball up into your little co-coon, gone, bye-bye, alone, away from reality, and then you become consumed in "fear for your life." You guess you could say in a lot of ways you hate yourself because of the thoughts you bring onto yourself. You think happiness for you is something as fictional and as nonexistent as this theme or discussion you just now extended into your noggin'. . . . And now you're sorry for that. More thoughts: To understand society's negativity, you must first understand how it's ran. Society is a machine, like all machines. Think if it as a car: A car's main job is to get from point a to point b. That means there's an entity giving it energy to do so. That energy is gas. Gas is the fuel to make the car keep running to be able to work until eventually it dies out. It's a cycle, over and over. This all being said, society is like a car. However, it's main objective isn't to get from point *a* to point *b*, no, it's to make the world around you run so-called "smoothly." But running smooth is an opinion. The fuel in this is money. Money is a point system we've created to put definite value into something. That value is "smoothness," whether it'd be art, entertainment, construction, services, et cetera. This society we have created is a tree with many, many branches. Cars are just a small twig in the big picture. The machine has to provide a service for us. But what seems to be a perfect system, it's not. Think for a moment whom you're dealing with: If there's definite rules that are created to be in place for this lovely, smooth, awesome world that the government or society deems to be perfect, it seems fine and dandy, right? But look at the fuel. The fuel is money. The entity, like the car, is us. But these are just machines, you see.

Humans are the issue in this equation. Most of depression stems from something greater, something underlying, something like an engine being broken. People like the idea of running smoothly, but they do not like the idea of work. People think that they are owed something. Look at the guy in McDonalds, working minimum wage, and look at the big CEO at some big company—they both are important, but in different ways. Both can be severely depressed and both can have very different things to be depressed about. The CEO could be worrying about getting a wife, and the CEO could be getting a bunch of gold-diggers, whatever. The McDonalds guy, like majority of society, like ninety-percent of society, is trying to find purpose and meaning in their life; you yourself know this one first-hand. The problems are endless, but lets look at the big picture: There's a family that loves to eat at McDonalds. The McDonalds guy is very minute in the family's life, but they don't realize that if he was never, ever there, they wouldn't have the luxury to just go up to a counter and ask for food and just hand over green paper and wait to be served. This society, the modern society, has become very efficient, but we haven't seen the life before all of it. We are spoiled. The CEO's job, though, is obviously different: he makes big decisions that the company must follow in order to succeed. These are just purposes. Some people feel the regular guy and the CEO are the highest and lowest value, but it really depends on how you look at the big picture. From the customer's point-of-view, we never seen the CEO, even though he is a big factor in the company's success. We always see the regular guy, but we think he's valueless because he's just like you and everyone else. But what people fail to realize is that the CEO is just like everyone else too. His job is not his value. But society has created this idea of value in very wrong places. Everything society runs by in America is capitalism, the idea of making something out of nothing. Everything you do in this world is based on being the one making the money, or being the one spending the money. Consumers vs. merchandiser. It's funny because it's all a game of cat and mouse. Sellers create advertisements and sneaky ways to get you to do things, while the consumers ask questions and want what's best for them. Sellers want money, and buyers want to feel accepted and happy. Both think that this is "happiness." Happiness is so not about material goods. But anyway, you guess you should get to the point: Depression's main problem just so happens to be insecurity, very generally speaking. Now, insecurity could be a number of things—how you look, how you speak, how you dress, how much money you make, et cetera—but ultimately it's your self-worth. Lots of people feel worthless. In fact, it's an epidemic. You ask yourself why society as a whole is so negative. So here's your answer: Value. The idea of value is bullshit. There is no pretty and ugly. There is no right and wrong way. There is no better or worse. There is no anything. It's all bullshit, it's all life. We forget the things we are grateful for. Take religion, for example. Religion is a great and powerful thing. Christianity—all that shit. The idea of people gathering around, really living in "the now" for once, is a wonderful thing. But yet again, capitalism and value creep their way into this equation, screwing it all up. That's why you choose not to go do that shit. Humans are honestly obsessed with self-worth. "If you do this, you will have this" is how we function now, which is very depressing. If you go into work every F-ing day, every freaking night, and work your friggin' ass off just to go home and watch the TV or look at your friends on Facebook showing off to the world of what they have that you don't, of course you forget about the things that you do have and you become depressed. You eat more, you gain weight, you do all these "bad" things to yourself, and yet, the very thing that deems them bad (value and capitalism) are the cause of it all. Who gives a flying fuck? Seriously. Just enjoy the things you have and work with what you got. People just forget. You know people want more, and that's fine, but it shouldn't be what consumes you. Obsession is not healthy. But you feel stupid and you feel like a hypocrite because you're talking about value here. It's often a touchy subject, but you yourself hope you get what you mean. You hope you answered your own question. You like the term "Going Bananas." It's weird as hell. You wonder who came up with the expression. Maybe a farmer. Anyway, that's what you've been feeling for a long time. Oh, god. One thing's for sure: you're going bananas. You have negative thoughts all the time. Reeeal negative. Sometimes you want to just punch and destroy every person on this earth, you get so negative. You understand what it must be like to be a terrorist or something. This overwhelming feeling of jealousy and hate toward others who seemingly have it better than you. And you just take it all away by force. It's wrong—you know—but it's all you can do in that state of mind. This state of mind swarms your F-ing inners. You're like a crying baby out in the middle of a super-highway, helpless, alone, no mom, no dad, nothing, just you and your un-walkable, helpless body looking up at the blazing sun and a huge semi-truck honking its horn and blazing down the highway, attempting to slow down for you, but—too late—splat, you die. This is what it's like. You hate it. You hate the world. We are all such savages. You feel like we all leech the shit out of everything. It's always "What's in it for me?" on their minds. And you're the very same way, but at least you're reserved about it. It's funny: if there's a problem, there's a solution. Sometimes it's a half-ass solution and sometimes it's full-proof. But someone is getting credit for it. You better believe it. And that form of credit might be money from your little wallet or purse. It's just so weird how the world operates. You have an issue going on that is not fathomable. Like it technically does not exist. It's thoughts. And in order to get help, a doctor tries to make money off of it by giving you meds, advice, whatever, then they'll have people calling you about it to collect it all, and make more problems for you, indirectly, and it would just be easier to keep your mouth shut. We are all such damn savage scums. This is your predicament and you hate it. You need to vent it all out. Your mom has told you not to do this stuff, like complaining to the world. But, mom, you say, you gotta vent it out! She tells you to get help, and the excuse cycle continues: you're broke, you hate hospitals, the help you get sucks, people don't understand, and the people that do know really can't do anything about it all. People tell you to smile. People ask you why you look so sad. You just wanna put a bullet in their heads when they say that. Not literally, of course, but it feels like it. You feel so small, so weird, so gone, so lost, so poor, so lame, so you, so crappy, so F-ing *stupid*. And don't tell yourself to get help because, nah, help is too expensive. And the people giving it have ulterior motives. It's true. Crap. You just wanna escape. That's why you paint, write, read. For escape. You just want to be gone. Everything is discouraging. You hate it. You hate it. Ugh. You just want to go home. This world isn't home. This world is a jungle full of tigers and lions and bears, and you're still a helpless baby. You just want your nonexistent utopia: going bananas. . . . So yeah, furthermore: You wonder what it is about women. They are the most greatest creatures on this planet, the most fascinating, the most loving (in your personal opinion), and the most outrageous. You wish you could understand them. Sometimes you just sit back and just watch them. Not in a creeper way, more in the sense of a scientist, tinkering with a mouse or gadget to see what it does. Sometimes you talk to girls in the matter of an experiment. It's weird. Sometimes you say the most loving things to make them feel good, but only to see what they look and act like. Sometimes you say the worst thing possible, and you hit deep inside their insecure spot, and they resent it, but it's weird because most of the time they forgive, but you best believe they don't forget. It's kinda like a grudge, in a way, which is scary. You love them. You really do. But they are a bit much on your brain. They excite you too damn much, but you never let them into your personal space. Mainly because you're scared of what they can do to you. They can make you do anything if you let them in, and you don't like that. You don't like the idea of something controlling you. Not in a man kind of way, but more in a freedom kind. But not in the freedom kind like rebellious. More in the way of not letting it be the wrong choice. That's really it. The girl is the choice. The one, the only one. Sometimes you think about being a Mormon, with, like, a thousand wives. Not in some pimpy pimp way. You just can't choose women for the life of you. They all are so wonderful and great. You love them all. They all make you feel good. There's not one that does more than the other. They all make you feel warm when they smile, they laugh, they talk, they joke, they walk, they hug, they kiss, they sashay, they love. OooOoo, the love they give is so damn warm! But you can't give the same love to just one. You always give less. Maybe you're selfish. Maybe this relationship stuff isn't for you. Maybe you're crazy. Or screwed-up. Maybe. This is what you think about when you observe one. The philosophy in this is real peculiar. Sometimes girls wonder why you don't just kiss them. Is it being scared? Is it being scared to be vulnerable? Sometimes you like to think it's because you don't want to force yourself onto them. When you get horny, you tend to overdo things: you pull hair, you moan hard, you grab, you throw them, you pin them, you lick, you bite, you go for the neck, you squeeze them, you just can't ever get enough. And it feels like you're a savage lion in the wild. It doesn't feel right. It feels like you're violating something, as weird as that friggin' sounds. They excite you too damn much. They are like a great, big teddy bear that you just want to cherish forever. They are so adorable and cuddly and warm and fine and great and wonderful and fantastic and smooth and soft and fragile and receptive and perfect. Everything about a women is perfect. Everything. Every woman has something about them that is special. And that's why you can't just pick one. They all make you feel this way. Sometimes you freak over one specifically, sure, but after you mingle and meet them and play "the game" and know them, you move to the next. It's all fun. You love it. It's not "player" to you because you provide a service to the woman. You want to give them the image of a good man. You want to be the image of a guy they want to be with. You want to show them how to be treated and loved and desired, because you've always wanted to feel what that's like, so you model what you think that would be like and that's why you know a lot of woman, but that's always why you're friend-zoned by quite a few of them. Not all, no, but quite a few. It makes you mad sometimes, but it makes you happy because it's easier for them to find a guy that they can be with for a pretty long time. Maybe it's weird to take all the credit. You don't know. But you'd like to think so. You just love women. You screw with them. It's weird that you're a virgin at twenty-one years old. Sometimes you have to lie about it because people don't believe you. You don't know. You just want a girl that can be something that you can be proud of, like your art, for example. Maybe that won't ever happen. Maybe all chicks aren't perfect. The girl in your head is the equivalence to the man a little girl pictures as the knight in shining armor—a fantasy. That's all. Maybe that's why you don't go for some chicks. Maybe you're looking for something that's a fairytale. That would be pretty depressing, you think. The idea of having a girlfriend (or boyfriend) is great and lovely and awesome and the best thing in the world, right? Everywhere you see advertisements that show how great getting married is, having kids, a home, the works, everything. Products know that we all want to be liked and loved, so they make things that make us think we can gain some security and love and be desired by all. You call this "Acceptance Advertisement." Even food. Beauty very obviously. But even food has some underlying presence of Acceptance Advertisement. Coffee: drink it, stay up, make money, buy more things you don't need, have things that people think make you cool, work hard to gain security for your future lover, whatever the case. But you think people are sick of it. And you think people secretly are embarrassed to be vulnerable with others about their faults. You think we all try and keep our minds busy with false confidence. Like flashy clothes, flashy cars, money, beauty, blah blah blah blah blah. The point you bring to yourself now is the fact that you see all of this going on and you see no progress, no success, no love, and no real lives. You just see false lives and false people. Lately you see couples that meet each other (like friends, family, et cetera) and you see them in courtship-mode. (That's also another sub-topic with Acceptance Advertisement.) You see the two people putting such a best foot forward, and they should—don't get it twisted—but it's to the point where they almost have to change who they are to put that best foot forward. Then they start dating, kissing, having sex, yada yada, blah blah blah, right? Great! grand! wonderful! But they think they found love. They think just because they saw this cute piece of ass flaunting around, they have found the all powerful, all seeing love that their heart's desire. Are you right? Eh, somewhat. Not all relationships end badly, and you should always plan for the best that you get out of them, but lately you've been seeing people just treading water. Seriously. They will see each other, yes, they will talk, yes, they hope they are the one, yes, yes, yes, but they weren't ever real with each other. It's this little thing in the air when you see them talking. This little ulterior motive floating above their heads: "What's in it for me?" And that's what consumers are. We buy ourselves into a person almost quite literally. Have you ever bought something and, after buying it, you feel so damn guilty for doing it? You go up to the TV, the display, and you try it out, you flirt with it, you have the sales people tell you how great they are, just to hyped you up, and how much you need it, how much it will make your life easier, happier, and then you buy it. And then after all of this honeymoon shit, you find out it doesn't work right. It doesn't power on when you want it to. Its wires are broken. It's used, it's helpless, it's a wreck, it's lame, and that's what you've been seeing. Now, after explaining all of this to yourself, you're probably asking, Brain, why are you telling me this? Why is this even cool or relevant to me? It's not, Mr. or Miss. Consumer. It's normal. It's humans. It's observation. But you will use yourself as an example to this. For one, you really can't stand the idea of a girlfriend. Everytime you think about a girlfriend, you think about a person who is not your ideal, because for some odd reason you feel like this is settling. You look at the TV and you notice the flaws about it right away before buying it, then you move onto the next TV and find more flaws, then the next, then the next, then the next, next, next. Finally, no more TVs are left and they now have your money. What does this tell you about yourself as a "buyer"?

Maybe you have commitment issues. Maybe. Possibly. Or maybe it's something bigger. Maybe you want a fantasy, a perfect girl, a perfect body in front of you, a doll (not literally), a cooker, a cleaner, a person not ever mad, a person that can handle things, a person worthy enough to brag about. But then you think about yourself, _____, and you think about if _____ even deserves this "ideal". You think about your flaws and your mistakes and your laziness and your anger and your destruction and your depression and your everything negative, and you think about this ideal girl, and you think she deserves better because she's the ideal girl. Now everytime you see a hot girl from afar you always think that she can do better. You don't want to be another Buyer's Remorse to her. You don't want to be fake for her. You don't want to let yourself buy flashy things and flashy cars and have big truck loads of money because it's just not you, and she deserves better, she deserves that real flashy you. But you don't even know what "better" is. If "better" is the flashy clothes, the flashy cars, the big truck loads of money, and you hate that "better," you will probably be single for the rest of your life; caught in this little fantasy life of better and worse. This girl—whom deserves better—is getting the "better" that you hate. Maybe there's just no such thing as love or marriage or happiness for you. Maybe happiness is just something fake that we created. Maybe it's all shitty. You don't know. Maybe you're a complete bullshitter who needs to get over his egotistical self and go out and bag a fresh piece of ass like all your other male friends in your life do. Maybe you should find sluts and ease the pain. Maybe you should continue to act like you care about a girl when really you don't.

Maybe you should continue to be selfish. But whatever this is, it isn't good and it isn't right. This life is impossible to live in. You hate everything about our social structures and social gatherings and social value. You hate it all! But this one woman, this one thing, this one fantasy, swarms your mind every damn day. You'll bet that one day when you do find a wife you'll probably make her so insane, so insecure, so lost, so angry, that she will be forced to go into Buyer's Remorse because you're the most broken TV on the display, and every salesmen in the world is trying to sell you off because they don't want you in their store anymore. Maybe you should go back to your distributor and be written-off. You don't know. Or maybe she should move onto the next TV. Clearly that's what is happening, considering your screen won't even turn the F on. . . . Walking, walking . . . step, step . . . eyes look up and . . . Oh look! Trinity hotel! Wow. That felt like it was fast! You were day-dreaming, but it helped! Oh shit, look at the building's grandfather clock installed at the top of its roof smack-dap in the middle . .

.

5:33 A.M.

Woah. You can't believe how late it is—or how early it is, if you wanna get *technical!* The drunkness is going away. You don't feel like a million bucks.

You're walking down the sidewalk (still) on the left side of Flagler. You pass the Trump building, one you toured and saw as a little kid and saw business men rant and rave about how the name "Trump" sells so well. You pass another building, one that is black, and you remember skateboarding on it when you were in high school, a time of freedom, coasting down those stairs out front. God you hate being an adult.

You start to pass some seafood joint, but then hook a left down . . . You forgot the street's name. Oh well. You walk down it and Clematis is looming up ahead. Nobody's around. You walk around a couple planters and see Pizza Girls, a overly-expensive pizza joint you ate at with your brothers and sisters when you were a little kid. You remember having some of the sauce on the corner of your mouth when you bit down on your very first slice. You remember your sister laughing and saying how silly you were. But then she hooks the bottom of her white shirt in her hand and wipes the ruby-red sauce off your face, and it left a red smear on her tee. Those were the days.

You pass this triangle-type fountain and it's off because it always is after seven. It just shoots up water from the ground, and kids play in it. This you don't have much memories about. The only one that comes up is when you were five or six and you saw a kid slip and fall face-first when trying to do a summersault at full speed. He cracked his head open and died. His parents weren't even able to help him by the time he left this earth.

You see all the bars down Clematis and you remember all the drunkards that danced out in the streets or grabbed random girls' asses, regardless if the girls have boyfriends or are married.

You thought of them as pigs but then you realize that you do the same things. So you inadvertently see yourself as a pig. . . . And oh look, Pizza Luna, the shitty joint that pretends to be like Pizza Girls. You think this and smile because your friend Tom back in the day loved that place. You miss Tom. You wonder where he is or what he's doing right now. Probably sleeping. . . . Probably living.

The library is up ahead and you see off computer screens and no lights on. Just nothing. Silence. And you think it's just silent enough to read a book in the middle of this night and cry and laugh and do anything you want because you're alone and you can do that. You miss laughing and crying. You wish it could last forever.

You turn down Daytura and realize your feet hurt but you're almost at City Place. You see the bank on Daytura and you remember it differently. They remodeled and took away the bank out front, like a tiled ramp that is along the wall. And you remember grinding on it with your skateboard and being able to glide and feel the wind in your face. They took it out because it caused too many lawsuits because too many skateboarders were gettin' hurt and parents were suing. They took it out because the architecture wasn't worth the upkeep.

You keep going and you see a bright City Place up ahead, with the Christmas-style lights hanging over the train-like light posts throughout the sidewalks and streets. It twinkles and is entirely beautiful. The above apartments show bright orange rectangles here and there, meaning lights are on, meaning that maybe people are getting ready for their nine-to-fives.

You're walking down the big courtyard and people are staring at you like you're nuts because you have a now dry, flaking, chunky pool of vomit down the front-end of your shirt and a little bit down your legs. You don't care anymore. You smile and realize that you have nothing to lose anymore.

You pass a sign that reads, in a classy, curvy font, WELCOME TO CITY PLACE OF PALM BEACH, and you nod at it, thinking what a day what a day.

You pass the Panera bread that is across from Muvico, it having shadows inside moving back and forth with alert, focused work-ethic, putting up boxes, moving chairs or this or that. Mopping. Making. Giving food to hungry humans.

Up ahead is the parking garage. Yes! You're finally there! You realize you smell like ass and feel like it too. You walk inside the parking garage and then run! You run, run, run, and finally, real kid-like, you tag your car's hood by pressing your hand firmly against it.

You made it. You're alive (is that good?).

You get out your keys and unlock your car with the unlock button, *duh*. You lean down to your driver's seat once you open the door. You press the trunk button and it pops.

You walk around your car and open the truck. You keep it open, stop, look in, and take a sighing breather.

"I can't believe . . ." you say.

You lean in and grab your backpack, unzip it, and then get your extra change of clothes out. You unfold them. You look both ways and around you. There's nobody around; just cars. You take your pants and shirt off and yeah, you were "going commando" all day yesterday so you are completely naked. You grab the clean clothes but then stop and look around again, grinning deviously. It feels nice to be naked. You like it. You gyrate your hips around and look down and see your flaccid four and a half inch cock doing circles and spins and you think this is halar' 'lar'.

You stop your little dance and grab the clothes and put them on. First the shirt, because you want your dick to be out for as long as you can. Then the jeans. You frown, kinda. You go back into your bag and grab the bottle of Zephyrhills you packed earlier. You take a swig. Your mouth tastes like pure ass. You leave your vomit clothes on the ground. You're about to close the trunk but then, oh wow, you see a car charger laying behind a jug of antifreeze and a car jack. You grab the charger. Close trunk. Watch check . . . Oh wait, it's gone, you remember. Watch checking is just a habit to you.

You walk around your car and get on in. Your cabin is quiet. You unravel the car charger and plug the car-end it into the cigarette lighter jack thingy (you're not too sure what it's actually called) and then you take "your" dead phone out from your pocket and plug the charger's phone-end plug into "your" phone.

An Apple sign beams on "your" phone screen. You look at it but then throw "your" phone in the passenger's seat. . . . You're just very exhausted. You wanna sleep. But before you do, you look at your console and the digital clock on it reads

6:09 A.M.

but you're pretty indifferent. You take another swig of your water and then close it and put it back to your lap. You just fall asleep and hope and pray the clock reads the afternoon. You hope all is going to be okay. So you just stare at the clock and shut your eyes, lying down in the—

9:03 A.M.

is what you see when you open your eyes and wake up to the sound of a key poking your windshield, *tap tap tap*.

"_____!!" Shelby's cute voice howling. "Open up!"

You go, "Uh, okay . . ." and Shelby, looking heated, walks around the back of your car and goes and opens your passenger-side door, hopping in. She sits, folds her arms, and just brutally stares at you. . . .

Awkward.

"Uh . . . hi," you finally say.

"What the hell is the matter with you!" Shelby yells. So much for peace and quiet.

You press your hands to your ears and say, "Jeez! Don't yell! I'm super hungover."

She bangs her palm on the back of your head, *whack!*

"Hey!" you say to her. "Stop!"

"No! You're an asshole!"

"How the hell did you find me?"

"Rob dipped out during the fight and he kept saying you had his phone. You have my purse so I went to your car." She looks down at her feet and leans forward and slings her purse over her shoulder. "What the hell happened?"

"I don't know," you say.

"Did you really kiss Connie?"

"Yes. But she forced it. Remember when she took me behind the stage at the concert?"

Shelby nods.

"Well, that's when she kissed me."

"______, you didn't want to?"

"No. I only like *you*, Shelby. You're my dream girl."

"And you're my guy. That's why I'm upset."

"I know, it's just crazy to me that we just met and I have these kinds of feelings for—"

"Did you really drink that much?"

You nod.

"Wow, ______. You gotta slow down."

"I'm just upset about everything."

"But why, boo?"

"Because."

"Because . . . ?"

"Because I hate my life, dude."

"You're a great person though, ______."

"Another thing too, Greg's sister and you in love, and Greg dating Connie, and Connie cheating with Greg, and the whole mix up. I don't know. It makes me mad."

"Trust me, it makes me mad too."

"I love you, Shelby, I really do. I would never cheat. Look at you! You're so sexy and smart and awesome. I'd never."

She grins. "Really? You love me?"

"Yes, Shelby, I really, really love you . . . a lot."

"I love you too!" She lunges a hug onto you.

"Ouch, baby." Your head hurts. "My head hurts."

"Aw, poor baby," Shelby says, purposeful pouting. She kisses your forehead. "Promise me, _____, that you will take care of me."

"I will. I always will."

"But you wanna kill yourself . . ."

"I don't even know anymore."

"You shouldn't, baby. You're really great."

"I think you're really great too. I just feel so shitty about myself."

"Hey." She locks eyes with you. "You're my guy and you're the best. You're confident, sexy, sweet, smart, awesome, and I love you."

Your face feels hot and you start to feel warm inside. You feel a small tear drop slide out your eye and down your cheek.

"Are you crying?" Shelby asks you.

"Yes."

"Aw. Don't cry, baby. It's okay."

"I just feel lucky to have you."

She goes silent, then finally says, "Lets go to my place."

You ask her, "Are you sure?"

"Yes."

"Okay."

"I really, really wanna make love to you, ______."

"I'm scared. You're so pretty. I'm a virgin. I've never even *seen* a naked girl."

"It's okay. I'll go slow." She smiles. "I'm glad I came here. Woo! Ha-ha-ha-ha-ha-ha!"

"What's funny?"

"I was gonna whoop your ass!"

"Jeez. Glad you didn't! Ha!"

"You're really cute."

You sigh. "Enough with the compliments. Lets ride."

"My knight in shining armor."

"Bes' believe it, suga!"

Shelby's smile it like a thousand beautiful sunsets or some corny shit like that. Smiley face.

You look at "your" phone and see there's over a hundred text messages, all from Shelby. You look up at her and she says, shrugging, "I wanted to get a hold of you."

You laugh.

Key in ignition. Shelby puts her purse down. Shelby's leaning into you and hugging around your arm. Reverse. Get out of parking garage. Wow. Clocky clock right there in front of you.

9:11 A.M.

Forget trying to hold it in. You really, really wanna have sex with Shelby. Look at her: she's tan, has probably D cups, ass for days, super funny, super nice, super down for you, has no drug problems, has her own life goin', has a job, wants to have sex with you, probably has a wet pussy right now, is in love with you, cares about you, wants you to succeed, and this all excites the shit out of you. So you get a huge hard-on.

Without even mentioning it, Shelby comments on it, saying, practically whispering, "I want that in me, baby," and holy shit, that's hot! So you grin and push on the gas and blaze down Dixie and cut a sharp left into Shelby's neighborhood. She keeps saying, "Baby, I'm so horny I want you baby I want you oh my god," and you say, "Almost there." She is fiendin' for you, bro.

Her house is up ahead. You're speeding. You stop on a dime in front of her house. You set the car in park and Shelby immediately gets out. You turn the car off, pocket "your" charged phone, and get out too. You want her so bad. You pull "your" phone out and check the time.

9:22 A.M.

Your boner is raging like a mother-frick. Shelby is walking up her house's pathway. You run up and spin her around and start forcefully kissing her. She wraps her arms around you, and she and you are walking to her front door, her backward, you leading. You both are still kissing and walking up the steps. You pin her against her blue door. Her hand is shaking because of how excited she is, and she is wobbling the door and not opening it. You stop your kisses and twist the doorknob because you wanna just get inside. She's all over you with her arms touching your upper body.

Inside, she's leading, and you're walking backwards while you both kiss. Both her hands are tugging the collar of your shirt to pull you against her. You feel her big, big tits leaning against your chest. She leads you into the living room. A dog barks. You both don't care. You guys bump into a sofa and stop kissing and you both laugh. "This is awesome," you say. "I know, right?" she says back. More kissing . . .

. . . this leading to her bedroom, it having a sign on it that reads NO BOYS ALLOWED, and this makes you wanna roll your eyes and laugh but you don't because you have a hot chick in front of you and she is opening the door, going on in, still kissing you, and is pulling on your shirt to push you toward her—

"Bed," Shelby says to you. "Now."

"Okay."

She is standing there in the middle of her room and you prop your upper body up with your elbows so you can watch her. She's so pretty. She has a black Daft Punk shirt on, super tight-fit, and these skinny jeans that hug her heart-shaped ass perfectly. She crosses her arms and pulls from the bottom front-end part of her shirt and pulls it off and over her head. She has a cute pink bra on. Her cleavage is very deep and full and nice. They, the boobies, are like two melons being cradled.

"You like these, baby?" she asks, pointing at them, then caressing them.

You are looking like the cartoon dog with his tongue out, slaving over her. You nod.

She giggles. "Good. All yours, baby." She gyrates her hips in a circular motion and turns around. You can see her pant-wearing ass and the pink strap of her bra around her back. Your dick feels like it's twitching.

She reaches behind herself and her fingers are pinching the bra strap and unhooking it. It snaps and goes undone. The straps both dangle. She turns her head over her shoulder and simpers. She then turns back around and is holding the bra up with both her hands.

"Do you wanna see them?" she asks.

Hell yeah you wanna see them! You nod! Gosh you wanna screw her brains out. This is like some porno shit to you. Is this even real life right now? It is. Ha-ha, man, oh man!

She tilts her head playfully and says, voice all high and sweet, "Okay!" Her hands drop forward and the bra falls off and, wow . . . there's no way to describe these jugs. They are so damn magical. Okay, okay, they have these small pink nipples and they are hard and pointing and very suck-able. No bumps of brail on them. You're wondering if they're fake. They are honestly a perfect round and shape. Like two of your heads. Massive and plump and full and so freaking FRICK! Oh my god, you can take it anymore.

"I wanna titty-fuck you," you finally admit to her.

"What?"

"Uh, I'm sorry. It was my first thought."

"It's okay. I'll let you. I want you to. Just take it easy." She smiles. She starts walking toward you and then leans forward on the bed and puts her knee at the edge and crawls toward you like a goddess. Her tits are hanging and they don't move. They are staying put as she crawls. Down her back you can see two curved hills of ass cheeks.

"Are those real?" you ask her, referring to her tits, not her ass.

"Yes! Duh, silly!" She giggles. "Touch them." She props on her knees, grabs your hands, and forces them to grope her big, big, plump, perfect jugs. . . . Wow. They are so totally real. They feel firm and the skin is so soft like silk and you are pinching her nips between your index and middle fingers.

She moans with her head back, her hair draping down. "Oh yeah, yes, b-baby. Oh my g-god." Then she looks back at you like a horny animal and pushes you and you fall back and she gets on top of you. Her knees are pinning your arms. You can feel her ass on your pant-covered dick. With her index finger, she lifts your shirt slowly. You start to feel a cold rush of air. You're not used to being naked.

"Sit up, baby," she says. "I gotta take your shirt off."

"Okay," you say. "Just be careful."

She grins. "I will, I promise."

"Okay." You grin and sit up.

"I love you, ______."

"I love you too." And you mean it.

You have your arms up and she pulls your shirt over your head and tosses it over her head and it goes wherever.

"Oh my god," she says, eyes wide, "look at your muscles! your abs! Oh my god, you're so *hot.*" She starts feeling your pecks.

"Really, Shelby?" You feel embarrassed. "I'm not all that great."

"And tan too! You are so built. I had *no* clue."

You laugh. "Thanks, babe. I'm glad you like my body."

"Like it? No, hun—I *love* it."

You grin and scratch your head. "Ah, shucks."

"Don't be so bashful!" she says, flirt punching you. Then she pauses and hugs you. "You're so awesome, ______."

You almost wanna cry.

"Baby, I gotta tell you something," Shelby, the love of your life, says. "It's important."

"Okay. What's it about?" You're concerned. "Lay down, boo."

She drops and lays down on your left arm. You wrap it around her soft body. She's a sweetie pie, you think. Her nose is just under your chin. You're looking up at the ceiling. She's got her hand on your chest, very snuggled up to you, as close as possible. Her left leg is over both your legs. Her forehead is leaning on your left cheek. She starts with "Don't interrupt me, I have a story to tell you" and you gently nod without bumping your chin into her nose. You'd never wanna hurt her. She starts talking. Here's gonna be a long one:

"This is really tough for to say," she starts, "but here I go. . . . So, um, I have dealt with a lot of assholes in my life. One in particular stands out to me. I didn't just become lesbian. I dated a few guys before. Some were nice and some not so nice. This one guy, his name was Aaron. Aaron was a drug dealer. . . . I know, I know, I met a buncha keepers. But anyway, Aaron met me at high school. He was a jock with straight A's and he always was very nice to me. We flirted a lot in class and one day he asked for my number. So I gave it to him and he started texting me.

"Days pass," she keeps going, sighing a bit, "and yeah, I went over his house and dated him. He was so sweet to me and did really nice things for me. We would smoke weed together and everything and he always made sure to compliment me and tell me he loves me. I told him I love him too, but I know now it wasn't really love, _____, it was lust. I thought he was really cute and hot. Mega hot. I remember we once watched Cinderella and, while massaging my feet, he told me he would totally look around for me to find the glass shoe that fit. I kissed him a lot. It was sweet, I thought.

"After a while, though, he started to get really weird. He was always shouting for no reason at all to me. Like he would always ask me, 'Where are you going?' and I'd be like, 'Just to my friend Sophie's house.' He would tell me no, and that I can't and that I don't love him. I would stay. Then he would do this weird yelling, and one day I was watching TV on his bed and he comes in the room and asks me, 'I wanna have sex.' I said that I was tired and I didn't want to and I told him I wanted to cuddle. I had my arms out to him and smiled. Then . . .

"Oh my god, I feel bad. This hurts so much to say, _______," Shelby chokes up a sec, tears going down her cheeks and you, right away, start to wipe them and tell her that it's okay, baby, it's okay. She keeps going on, saying, "He told me that I . . . that I didn't love him if I didn't have sex with him. So I told him no and that I *did* love him. He said that if I even remotely loved him then I would have sex with him. But I was a virgin. I wasn't ready, in all honesty. But I agreed to it to make him happy. I didn't wanna make him mad. He was already balling a fist and looking down at me while I was lying on his bed. I said, 'Just take it easy, baby. Be nice,' and he said, 'Yeah, yeah, okay, sure, whatever,' and he was leaning over and started to be really rough. He p-pulled . . ." She stops. She's crying. "Oh-oh m-my god, I'm so ashamed, _______! It hurt so bad!"

"What did he do?" you asked her, more heated than you've ever been in your entire F-ing life.

"He pulled my shirt off and then pushed me on my back and grabbed my jeans from the ankles and really yanked them off. I was just in my bra and underwear and I was covering myself. He told me that he wants to see my boobs. He told me he wanted to s-suck them. So he jumps and gets on top of me and pulls my bra off from the front and my strap tore from the back and gave me, like, a paper cut. It hurt really bad. I was scared. But then he started to take his shirt off and he had gym shorts on and I could feel is penis lying over my crotch. It was really big and scary. He told me to touch him and I wanted to say no but I was way too scared so I touched him anyway. He told me that he knew I wanted him and then he rolled his gym shorts down over his penis and then yanked my underwear off. I closed my eyes and pretended I was somewhere else, far, far away. I wanted it to end as quick as possible. I kept thinking that this wasn't the way I pictured having sex. It was brutal.

"Anyway, we were both naked and he spread my knees and said, 'I know you want me. Say you want me, baby,' and I said yes, but my voice was going small. He said, 'Good,' and then he pointed his dick and put the whole thing inside. _____, you have no idea how bad it hurt! It felt like lightning and eels had stung me it hurt so bad. I was bleeding but he didn't even look down. He just kept staring at me and grabbing my breasts and he kept, like, humping me. I was so scared. It hurt so bad. So I started to cry. He asked, 'What's wrong?' and I said, 'Nothing,' and he screaming in my face, 'No! What! Is! Wrong!' 'Nothing!' I said back. Then, weirdest thing, he slapped me, hard, across my face! I held it and then he kept humping me and kept telling me to enjoy it and he's almost done. Then he quivered and said he was cumming inside of me and then he held my shoulders and later, left bruises on them.

"He came inside of me and then got up off me and I was crying. He was standing and telling me to be quiet. He was putting his pants on. I was still crying and he said, 'Hey!' then grabbed me from the bed and stood me up. He was in my face, all like, 'You should feel lucky.' Then I was telling him he hurt me and then he shoved me really, really hard on the floor, and as you can see, my room has tile floors! I was hurt so bad. I hit my head and he said, 'You're so lucky that's all I do to you.' And then he said, 'Talk to me when you're normal again,' and then he walked out of my room and drove away. I was devastated!

"Then I think, like, a couple weeks later I was getting sick 'n' stuff and Tessa told me to take a pregnancy test and I found out I was pregnant. I didn't tell my parents and then—"

"Wait," you say, stopping her. "How long ago was this?"

"Umm, about, uh, high school."

"Okay. Keep going."

So she does, like, "Yeah, and then I had to go to the abortion clinic and use some of my savings that I was gonna use for college to fund this. I got the abortion and ever since then I felt like a killer and a victim. I always felt like shit. So I dated women. Women are really nice. They have soft skin, they are gentle, they would never hurt me, and yeah, I love them. But once you came into my life today, you showed me I could love men again. It was really great. So that's why I wanna have sex with you. That's why I turned you down at the beach because I had conflicting feelings about the idea."

"I see," you say, holding back tears.

"Baby?" Shelby is concerned, you can tell by the sound of her voice. "It was a really long time ago."

"You were raped. I'm pretty upset."

"I see. Well, it's okay, I guess. It was a horrible thing for me but I came to the conclusion that it doesn't change the person who I am. I'm still me."

"I love you."

"I love you too, _______."

A smile widens on your face. "I'm glad you told me this story, Shelby," you say.

"I'm glad too. You're the only person I've ever told."

"I'm mad you were hurt." You're rubbing her shoulder.

"There's just some messed-up people in this world."

"I feel like I'm one of them sometimes."

"Why's that? I don't think so."

"Well . . ." You laugh. "That's because you like me."

"I know!" she laughs. "Do you have any secrets?"

"I have my lovely bear share."

"Bear share?"

You nod, thinking that was weird to say.

"Isn't that a download whatever-thingy?" asks Shelby, the lovey love love.

You laugh. "I'm just weird. Basically all my relationships have consisted of me being awkward."

"Why are you?"

" 'Cause I'm not okay with myself. I just wanna be loved."

"You gotta love yourself, _______, in order to—"

"—to be loved," you say, completing her sentence. "Been told it all."

Shelby moves her head up, sits up, faces you, on top of you. "I think you're really great."

"Everything's gonna be, um, okay, Shelly," you say, unsure, trying to butter her up.

"You're sweet," she says back, probably thinking that your facial expression is sweet and not in fact having actual doubts in your head of her.

"So . . ." you start, "what now?"

"Lets *do* it." She grins. "Yeah?"

"Can I get a condom from my car?" you ask, knowing it makes no sense that a virgin would have one.

"Yeah!" She totally doesn't catch the idea.

"Okay," you say. "Be right back."

"Baby," she says, then kisses you. "Be back fast. I'm very wet."

You feel your dick hurt because your pants are in the way. "Do I smell?" you ask, thinking about how you haven't showered in a while now, and considering you vomited on yourself earlier.

"Um . . . Honestly, a lil' bit." She shrugs. "But it's okay! Just come back. We could do it in the shower."

You look at her boobs.

"And yes, _____, you get to play with them." She rolls her eyes, smiling. She's a peach, ain't she?

She talks about herself, you think, while you look up at her round clock on the upper wall over her door and its longer hand spins fifteen times, but you're not really looking at the time, and then you interrupt lil' Shel Bel.

"Be right back," you put her to her side of the bed, taking her off the top of you, and it makes you sad.

"Be back, baby," she keeps saying to you.

"I will," you mutter.

You stand up, without a shirt, just your pants on and socks and shoes. You grab your shirt on the ground. You walk over to her bedroom door, it still being open, and you walk out, closing it behind yourself. You hear a sigh behind the door and a voice talking to itself, like, "Gosh, Shelby, you outdid yourself." You grin. Never had a chick be *that* into you like that.

You're looking all around the room. It smells like Febreze, the orange Hawaiian-scented kind. There's a couple family photos but nothing too crazy. Just a dad, a mom, and Shelby. They look happy in their little poses. Shelby looks young. She still looks really adorable, even back then, you think. You put your shirt back on.

You walk forward and there's a desk. On it, there's small drawings and paintings. There's one of a small duck floating on a lake. Looks like one you fished at, caught a few shit, then left. You're thinking dull thoughts dully. Another is of a landscape and it looks very blue. In fact, majority of the paintings are blue, mostly. You see a painting that looks like it just has a blue base on it. It's just solid royal blue. It's big. You wonder if this is Shelby's doing. You see a few sticky-notes. You take one sticky note, a pencil, and you scrawl on the sticky-note, TWENTY-FOUR HOURS TO LIVE. I WANT TO DIE. I HOPE YOU SEE WHAT I WANT TO DO. I LOVE YOU. BYE and then you place it directly in the middle of this blue-based painting and it looks so divine, though you're wondering why you did that.

You look both ways: the way to Shelby's room, or the way out the door and to your car. You choose the car way. Why? You don't really know. You're not too sure if you deserve love. You really don't love yourself, none the slightest.

Out the door, passed the front lawn, into your car, you see your clock. It's there. Oh.

10:01 A.M.

You are starting to think that of all the clocks you've seen all day, none of them could've been accurate. Oh well. . . .

You sigh then start your car. You feel very bleak. You're asking yourself why you're leaving Shelby, a girl who wants you, who needs you, who *craves* you, and you wonder why you feel so ashamed in yourself. Maybe it's the idea that this guy raped her and by you having sex with her it, um, would just be a burden for her. . . . You think about how people would tell you that you're crazy, you're nuts, but you don't care, whatever. . . .

You start to drive aimlessly. You start to think, This is it. And you know where you want to do your little act. You think about how you want to die. Not by a knife, that's too painful and you could back out easy. Not by drowning, you would freak out and couldn't breathe and you would struggle for air, though it would be the most peaceful way to go, sitting there under the water and seeing clear blue as you slowly drifted to whatever after-life their is . . . or isn't. . . .

You start to drive but you feel like laying down and going to sleep; possibly with a hot chick, a chick who wants to have sex. But you blew that chance. So yeah, depression hits. It always does. . . .

Going slow down Dixie you vaguely glance out the window and you see a woman being mugged by some hooded dude and they're grabbing and tug-o'-waring, you assume, her purse. You think about helping her, but then you don't. You keep going. . . .

Shit. You're almost on E. Both you and your car. You're pretty F-ing hungry, but also too tired to care. You pass Howley's, a restaurant you thought was kickass when you were a little boy, and you wanna stop for a burger. . . . "Your" phone is buzzing a loud, humdrum, urgent, shrill jingle. It's Shelby—go figure. It just rings constantly so you silence "your" phone by shifting the tiny lever on its side and then your screen flashes a big bell with a line across it, basically telling you you won't hear from that bitch never, ever again.

Skkkirrrrrrrrrt! you sharply turn on into the front parking space at Howley's. A wall in front of you is painted with two obscure, tangled waitresses carrying trays with beer on them, their eyes wide and bug-eyed like an alien's, like you right now. But you don't sweat it, you're getting out of your car now. The dumper smell of grease haunts the fresh, open Florida air. . . .

You're walking and walking and, oh gosh, you see these two girls walk passed you, the ones from yesterday by Muvico, and they grimace at the fact they see you, probably because maybe you're a stalker? you think. But then you don't think and you pass on by them, hoping they don't look you up on Facebook, the current social media site you're on, or something. . . .

You want to go inside but then you stop right before the entrance and look over at the outside tables; they are oldish and withered like this one guy's house you knew named Doug who your dad visited years ago to "hang out" with but years later you found out Doug was selling drugs to him, the F-ing low-lifes. So you walk over to the table, dust the specks of cig butts off the seat, look up at the blue, crystal-clear blue sky, and you sit down, immediately leaning your head forward into your hands, not crying, not thinking about anything in particular, and you sigh that deep breath of relief that this life is going to finally be over and done with. . . .

A husky, fat husky man with black Wayfarers, an Armani suit, and two hookers at both sides of him with his arms over their shoulders walks by, and you ask him, trying to be as friendly as possible, "Hey man, what's the time, d'you know?" "Piss off, kid," he says back, probably on a roll. Then he walks on in. You bury into your hands and a tear actually comes out. After a few moments of this, of crying your life away, a finger taps your shoulder, and you look up.

Out of seemingly nowhere is a boy, about eight, hair curly, eyes big, glasses on, pretty tall for his age, shirt like Where's Waldo?, shoes two sizes too big for him, ears all out like Dumbo's, shorts that are cut-offs, and this boy says, careful not to upset you more, you think, "The time is . . ." He trails, then pauses, maybe trying to figure out the time. And then he says it.

10:12 A.M.

"Thanks," you sniffle, looking up at the boy, and you're thinking if his time is actually accurate.

"You're welcome," he says, all cutesy and nice-like, then, sitting down at the seat next to you, his legs crossed, his elbows on knees, him leaning, looking at you, into you, "You okay?"

"Yeah, I'm fine, just depressed is all." You say it like you know the kid. Then you look back at your hands like they are someone else's.

"Why are you . . ." the kid starts, "um — I don't know — sad?"

"What?" you say. "Spit it out, kid."

So he does . . . like, "Crying. I mean, why are you crying, sir?"

This makes you upset. "You mean sobbing!" Your tears are coming out from some land you know nothing of, and it's pretty F-ing lame and gay, you think.

"Oh," the kid simply says.

You sniffle again. "Kid, what's your name?" you ask. "I'm sorry I'm sorry. I'm just goin' through some shit."

The kid doesn't say anything, he just stares.

"Oh, uh, sorry," you apologize for no reason at all. "I, um, shouldn't curse; you're really young." You pick up your right leg and cross it over to the left, thinking how this makes you look like a proper adult, or whatever the heck that is.

He still stares and you think, God, the madness! So you just explain.

"Kid, I know I don't know you, but just listen, okay?"

He nods, deathly listening to each word you're saying, surprisingly.

"Okay, kid," you say, licking your lips after. "Um, so, about three months ago I decided I wanted to kill myself. Most people think it's nuts and probably shameful. But I don't care.

"And anyway," you keep going, "I woke up yesterday with the intent to kill myself in twenty-four hours. I'm just shy of, um, two hours left to go. I'm nervous. I'm scared. I'm everything unpleasant. But nothing's changed and—"

"Uhh," the kid interrupts.

"What?" you say.

"Why would you do *that?*" The kid's voice is really high. It's like a helium balloon. It's actually pretty cute, but not in a pedophile kind of way.

"I guess I just don't see anyone getting me," you answer. "I just sort of do things and everyone just looks at me funny."

The kid doesn't say anything.

"Like you are right now," you tell him. You're almost feeling more in tears.

The kid goes, "Well . . . I'm listening, but I don't get it!"

"It's okay," you sigh, scratching your head. "You're young."

"My papa says that bad man do bad things, but you don't seem like a bad man."

This makes you smile. "You think?"

"Absolutely!"

"Wow, kid, thanks."

"Why don't you eat ice cream," the kid says, excited. "Always makes *me* happy!"

You laugh. "Ha-ha. You're cute, kid. Where's your pops?"

"My what?"

"Your pops . . . You're *dad,* I mean."

"Oh! He's inside."

"That's cool."

The kid stands up, saying, "I just came out here to go to my dad's car and give him his smokers."

"You mean cig*arettes?*" you laugh.

"Yes!" The kid laughs too. "Smokers! Then I saw that mean man yell at you and it made me sad."

"Thanks, kid," you say. "You're sweet."

"Mhm," he says, nodding. "Don't mention it. But hey, I gotta go back inside. It was nice meeting you!"

"Nice meeting you too," you say, depressed, bored, irritable.

"Hey," the kid suddenly says, staring serious but positive into your eyes, "I just want you to know, sir, that you shouldn't feel so sad! The world is really fun. I know I'm just a kid and whatever, but my daddy tells me I'm the smartest boy on the whole, wide planet. Just wake up and tell yourself it's a new day. Believe in the big man up stairs, my daddy says. I think you should believe in something like that! It's really magical! Like *Aladdin!*"

You smile and tears actually come out. So you say, "Thanks, kid."

"Just be good," the kid says. "Bye!" Then he walks around the table and skips happily toward Howley's entrance and opens it and goes on in, living his care-free life, the little rascal.

You reflect on what this young kid said. Wow. So wise. You think he's right. Maybe you should appreciate what your creator has given you, whatever it is, whatever *He* is.

10:23 A.M.

So, um, yeah. You get up and walk inside Howley's. The door squeaks like hell. A bell rings after you close it behind yourself. There's a bunch of old dudes, forty-ish in age, hanging out by the bar, which is the first thing you see when walking in. The dudes are all laughy and one of them looks at you suspiciously, mean-muggin' you.

You look up at the TV that hangs above all the liquid ethanol bullshits and the TV, all square and boxy and not HDizzle, has the News on, not sports or ESPN, and the News is talking about how last night at Dr. FeelGoods there was a Redbull girl that got so drunk she was handing out Redbull to people in the middle of Flagler and got hit by a semi, head on, and died instantly, whatever. And you think, What if I went and stopped her? Would she have lived? Would she?

Honestly, you're totally tired, exhausted, everything, through the hazy, glorified sobriety that has now fully fallen over you; but it has not with the old men next door, you figure. Your drunkenness was replaced with "not drunk anymore" and your "not drunk anymore" was replaced with heavy eye lids, a broken feeling in your heart, unsureness, a need for sleep, and, of course, sadness and depression. You sit at the bar table, listening to the light humdrum of chitter-chatter as it clammers its way, almost very hypercritical and mini-critical of you personally, into your soul like a piercing, slamming, voluminous whale dick of hatred. So you ask the bartender for a beer by giving the ol' raise of a hand and he nods and knows what it means, all with his white towel over his shirt and cleaning a glass in a very cliché type of '50s way. . . . A hand touches your shoulder.

"Hey, can I get'cha anythin', sweetie?" a waitress, thick at the hips, skinny at the waist, voluptuous at the tits, black-shirted, says, with her name-tag, you notice, reading KATIE SWOOP.

"Nah. No thanks, doll-face," you say, not grinning, not smirking, saying it pretty casually without hints of flirtation.

"What?" she says, unbelieving.

You look into her eyes. "I. Want. Nothing."

Her eyes squint. "Don't I know you from somewhere?"

"Probably."

"You look like my future ex-boyfriend!" And she giggles, knee-slapping. "Then name's Katie!" She holds out her knee-slapping hand.

"I know," you inform her ass, "I can read," and you point at her tag, passing and not shaking her hand.

"Jesus. Just tryna be nice," she says. Then the kid, the one that was talking to you about twenty minutes ago, walks passed her, behind her, down the aisle, and he sits next to some older guy, about forty-ish, like the guys at the bar, and the kid sits next to the forty-ish guy and you think it's a father and son, peas and carrots. "Well, gosh, are you even listening?!" Katie grimaces. "Ugh," she loudly sighs, then walks off, doing her thing, her thing with looking hot and purposefully flirting with random men just to gain a buck.

You turn back around and there's a healthy mm-mmm bottle of Dos Equis right there in front of you. So you grab it and put its cap to your armpit and squeeze and twist, popping it open. The cap drops to the floor and you raise the bottle up, gulp gulp, and, *ahhhhhhh*, sigh like a champ, but depressive-like, obviously.

Your eyes are darting all over the place: a billion, zillion paintings etched out of bullshit acrylic on canvas from posers big and small; the remains of bowls with half-eaten food still in them that those "hungry" Americans could've taken home, though they forget that children starve around the world for just a fraction of their leftovers, a small morsel to share amongst the open village; a trophy for a soccer championship that, hey, you remember Robert was at and you saw him win it with flying colors; more food; two lovers picking at spaghetti with their forks and looking like, mimicking like, *Lady and the Tramp*, with them having the noodle dangle between their lips from both its ends and the Pacman-style nom, nom, nom just before they reach for their saucy kiss, the bastards; a plant inside something like a . . . surfboard? you guess; and a bartender telling you to stop spilling on the counter, sir, and him snapping his fingers at you.

"What!" you blurt, coming back to reality. "Oh shit, man, I'm sorry." You look at the counter and your beer is toppled over, its liquid pooling, lapping out, waterfalling over the counter.

"Sir, are you gonna pay for this?" the bartender, leaning forward in front of you, says to you in a tone loud enough for others to hear, staring dead at you, his hands on his side's edge.

You go, "Uh, uh . . . uh . . ." and then stand up and everyone is looking right at you, even the little boy you talked to.

"Again, sir, are you gonna PAY for this?" the bartender repeats, more louder, creating a scene.

You turn around and bolt for the door, leaving.

Behind you, the door slams and you can hear it as you run toward your car, caring no fricks.

You start laughing. You bring out your keys and butt-slide over your car's hood once you get to it. You perfectly execute the slide and get to your driver's side. You unlock, pull open, and hop inside the door's lovely escape route . . . sort of.

Passed the dashboard, passed the cracked, dirty, filthy windows of Howley's that need to be cleaned, you see heads looking out, some shaking from side to side, probably not believing what an asshole you are.

You look at the odometer and put your key in the keyhole and start the bitch, but then, *bam bam bam*, arms are pounding at your car's hood. It's the bartender. He's screaming.

"Pay, asshole! PAY!"

So you put your car in reverse, faster than you've ever done in your life, and you place your right arm over the back your passenger side's headrest, looking over your shoulder, and you step on the gas, turning out. Then more slamming happens but on your side's window. The face is clenching and enraged, still screaming full-on.

"I'm gonna *kill* you, kid! I'll find your ass!"

Vaguely, as you put your car into drive, you gun it, going straight, not stopping at the immediate stop sign that's there, and you turn right onto Dixie. Going as fast you can, seeing not a cop in sight, strangely, you think the bartender was F-ing nuts and overreacted just a little tiny bit. But then you think about the economy and, oh yeah, that was probably the owner, not just some whatever-whatever bartendertard. But no-sir-ee, you really can't be too sure. Fun time's over. City Place bound! Speed. Look down. Oh. Clock.

10:38 A.M.

Shelby is blowing up "your" goddamn phone, though! Holy shit you can feel it vibrate every five seconds, it seems like (but you're wondering if it's maybe other people besides her, considering it's Rob's phone). It's kind of pissing you off a bit. But no matter, off you blaze down the roads at a mere thirty-five mile an hour speed limit. The door of your car is wobbling and hitting something like a steel plate, and you're wondering about how much it costs for you to fix it. Maybe next week you'll . . . Wait. You're gonna die soon, you kind of think.

You stop at a stop light and have one hand at the top of your steering wheel like a gangstertard. So you get your AUX cord and plug it into "your" vibrating phone and see one-hundred and twenty texts from Shelby and then you click on passed them and go through "your" iTunes app and find, though you placed it there months ago, The Door's "Light My Fire," and play it. You bob, from within some deep positivity, your head up and down to the, you think, lovely music. The song plays but its volume is muting every couple seconds because Shelby is still trying to get a hold of you. The red light turns green and you press on the gas, going going, gone!

You wail out and sing, though honest and rather terribly, to the song playing glitch-like from its stops and text messages blocking the bicker and batter of, you honestly freaking think, awesome "tune-age" that you currently are crying from. There's actual tears and nothing seems like it's the way to go, the way to be, because the fat, waterfall fat gumdrop tears storming their way down your cheeks, your neck, your soul, your heart, and consume you with feelings of ominous guilt, madness, and down-right failure that no true human, or animal, could ever fathom through its wrenches of metaphorical happiness.

White Tops, the parking place that you skated when you were a sixteen-year-old, creeps up on you and memories of a forgotten time whoosh their way through your agony, pain, suffering, all that garbage, and they come at you, vivid and bright. The times of relaxation, gazing up at the blue cloudy sky and seeing airplanes pass over every now and again, you felt at ease and breathed in, while closing eyes, fresh Florida air and you felt exhilarated, even as the sounds of polyurethane wheels from skateboards clanged and banged on the cement after outrageously complex tricks flipped and twirled in thousands of different combinations. It was simple.

So you park your Civic at White Tops and, again, sigh instead of seeing it as a breath of fresh air, and you wince from your past exuding itself into the present's window of opportunity, the opportunity of backing away, canceling, and forgetting the messy mess of all your messes. You look in your backseat and see some Converse Chuck Taylor's that are red. You grab them and scoot your seat back and put them on your feet. You get out your car. You don't even lock it because you think, What's the point? So you throw your keys and they flip, one, two, three, four, and thump to the dead grass off to the side of this place. Your car's function instantly ceases use and swoons over your noggin', tenfold, becoming a must-be-trashed thingamajig, whatevs.

You're walking along White Top's sidewalk, down Okeechobee, and, to yourself, you're saying, "The one thing twice once for this ever to be blah blah is to forward over the conscious of poop in the flash flash okay boyo time ghost feel-it awesome car broseph in the agony of the love you never go on to receive once for this everlasting grief this is not right and I'm speaking like an asshole . . ." and you feel like you're going crazy.

"Your" phone rings. . . . You sigh and the reach into your pocket and press the accept button. You speak softly into the phone.

"Hi, Shelby."

She's pissed. "______!!"

"Yes . . . ?"

"Where are you?!"

"I don't know, babe. Where are *you?*"

"Stop. Where are you?"

"I'm walking down Okeechobee. I'm going to my old apartment building."

"What building?"

"The City Place Towers. It's just regular apartments."

"Why are you going there?"

You start to think about saying "Just to get my stuff from there, my old apartment, and move someplace else," but then you realize Shelby knows better, so you just say the truth by saying, "What d'you think?" even though it's just an insinuation.

"What do *I* think?" she says. "You better not kill yourself, ______." Vaguely you can hear her choke up on saying your name.

"Whelp, I'm going, going . . . back, back to Cali Cali, baby girl," you say, monotone, not at all sounding or singing like Biggie. You feel weird.

She doesn't get it. Putting her face probably closer to the phone, you assume because of how loud, how muffled, it's sounding, she says, words split up, "Don't—you—dare—*kill*—my man!"

You hang up and, oh look, it's

11:02 A.M.

and you're walking right passed Rosemary and Okeechobee, crossing toward The City Place Towers, your old apartment. You stare up at it as you step on the perfectly laid tan stone tiles on the sidewalk leading toward it. The rich need to step on gold, you think. But then you think it's stupid to assume that, considering you lived at Towers just like "them." Oh well. Upward you see pigeons at the top of the building and they're on its edge, shitting probably, the little bastards, and it makes you excited to see them up there! High up, from looking at this point, it looks like they're gods. You wanna prepare. So you pull "your" phone out and set an alarm for twelve o'clock, so you can know the exact time to off yourself.

Both ways you look down the street. You see a hand-holding couple walk by, laughing and giggling, with their bleach-white smiles and new clothes on, all by Gucci or whatever, and they walk passed you like nothing. You sigh and keep walking. Down Rosemary, on the West side of the sidewalk, you cut into an alleyway you have never seen before, or never noticed. It looks great and totally creepy and dark, which is what you're going for, so you walk down it.

You see steam from a water pump, trash from cans toppled, clothes on clothes lines up above, random shirts spilled with oil on the black tar ground, a flag pole of some sorts tap tap tapping its chain from the wind, and you keep walking and notice all this and think, This . . . is . . . it . . .

You can see a fire-escape staircase thingamabob, its steel all diamond-ed and criss-crossed, and there's a ladder that hangs straight down, strong and sturdy, and is about two feet higher than your head height. You walk up to that, the ladder, and look up. It doesn't look too big! You lower, crouch, and jump! You grab the bar and lift, lift, lift! Your chest is to the bar and your legs dangle. You vaguely look down and it already looks like you're high up. You keep lifting and now your knees are on the bottom bar and you're holding onto the third bar. You keep going up, up, up, until you're eventually into the fire-escape staircase.

Grabbing hold the handlebars, taking a deep, cautioned breath, halfway closing eyes, thinking about doing this, you step up the steps that spin in a squared spiral up toward the roof, and you do this and notice the "steppings" forever, in a delayed, numb way, coming up: step . . . and then, oh look, the roof. . . .

Hearing sirens off somewhere, not feeling "your" phone vibrate in your pocket, you know something is up. You pass the wall opening to go onto the roof. The ground or whatever over here feels rough under your feet and rubs together and grinds with gritty sandpaper of some sorts. . . . More sirens.

You start to take steps, but they aren't that big. You spread your arms out and feel the air rushing from being so high up. There's nothing really around on the roof—just generators, a door, the fire-escape staircase, whatever. You keep looking around and the sun is beaming down onto you. Maybe because the roofing is black. Up ahead, about a four foot wall circling around this roof stands.

You walk up to it, look both ways, see the triumphant sun, its garish sky around it haloing a golden ring, and you look over the edge of the wall. Green, red, blue balloons soar upward, passed you. You see them.

Down below—vertigo! vertigo! vertigo!—you can see cop cars, about five of them, parking panicky. Your visuals gyre and cyclone backwards and forwards, and you think, whilst noticing no F-ed gas smell of city permeating the air like usual, What the heck?

A cop, who looks like the cop that let you and Shelby and Rob go yesterday when he pulled you over for speeding because Shelby showed her tits and all that jazz, stands out from his car and has a huge megaphone and, oh God, his probably anodyne self prepares it by connecting the box thingy to it and he steps forward, being directly down from your sights, and says to you, in a huge megaphone-style call, "Don't do it, kid. It's not worth it."

Of course he would say that, you think, sighing. You shout down at him, with him now being surrounded by other cops, people, et cetera.

"YES IT IS, FAGGOT!!"

Okay, so you got cop over here with the megaphone, some faggot people down below starting to crowd or whatever, and then you got . . . Oh no! There's a purple car screeching down the streets and it parallel parks sloppily next to the cop cars like a crazy person.

Oh god, it's Shelby. *Crap!* No. She's down there too! She's running! Oh . . . your . . . *God!* Running up next to the cop. She's all close to him, next to his ear and he hands her the megaphone. Dear lord.

"_____, everything is going to be fine! Don't. Do. It! I love you."

With your hands cupped outward up to your mouth, you yell, "I KNOW, SHELBY, I KNOW! I LOVE YOU TOO!!"

"Get down from there!" she says.

"WHAT TIME IS IT?" though you have a phone in your pocket with it, but you ask anyways.

"I'm not telling you!"

Then the cop takes the megaphone from her hands, puts it up to his mouth, and informs you that it is

11:12 A.M.

The cop is rather curious-looking, though. Even this high up you can see his face crunch, and then he whispers into

Shelby's ear. . . . Hmmm. You imagine him asking her, "Why does he want to know the time, ma'am?" and her answering, "Because he wants to kill himself at twelve," but instead, the cop says, with his big, fat yellow megaphone, "It's going to be okay, sir, just . . . stay . . . calm."

This makes the sky seem to *bleh* and melt profusely into some form of blue shit, some tear drop, some bull that rams his huge dick into you, repeating, and makes you pay, but then you say, after a few seconds of this mind-numbing bullshit thoughts/pause, "I. AM. CALM!"

Shelby, taking the megaphone from the cop, ruffles it because of how nervous, how sad, how mad, how irritated, how scared, how terrified, she is, and then moves the mic to her mouth, blurting, "Rob is coming! He's coming with Tessa! Everything is okay, baby! Everything is okay!" Blah, blah, blah is all you hear from this bitch.

Spectators, big and small, ages ranging from, well, every age, come up in swarming, urgent crowds, gazing up, their heads back, in awe of this perfect little scene, commiseration probably F-ing gone from their noggin'. Maybe they're even, you guess, taking pictures? It's too high up to see.

You feel sick . . . obviously. Flash, flash, flash go the iPhones and gadgets and bullshits. Oh look, here is the day's show! . . . Screw you.

More Megaphone Shelby: "I'm so sorry, hun! I'm sorry I didn't help! I'm sorry you feel like this! I'm sorry!"

All the sorrys in the world don't, can't, help. You read the words smeared across dead trees, across billboards, across back-end of airplanes or blimps, and you realize, above all else, that you hate everything, you imperious, F-ed beezy you.

"I HATE EVERYBODY!" you scream downward, directly at these lame-Os.

A car, speeding, screeches and cuts on into the parallel parking spot next to Shelby, next to the cop. Two humans, male and female, good-looking, lame, awesome, in love, not even caring no hells, come on out of the car, hurriedly, and the male one is Rob; and you assume the female is Tessa, the college bitch he told you about yesterday before going to Shelby's house. They run toward the event at hand. Two dots, one with black hair and one with blonde, coming toward the plethora of dots, looking up.

The Rob dot, holding the Tessa dot's hand, is shimmying between the crowds until eventually, thank God, he comes up to Shelby and the cop.

"PISS OFF!" you shout.

The megaphone is, again, handed off, and that hand off is now to Robby-Rob.

Looking up, pointing the megaphone up, Rob announces, "Oh lookie, we gotta jumper!" and then you hear him laugh. The mic muffles and then Shelby takes it away, putting it up to her face.

"Don't listen to him, _____," she says. "He's not a friend!"

He never was, she's right.

Rob takes the megaphone back, saying, "I'm just messin' with ya, man! Come down, dude! It's not that serious!" but then the cop snatches the mic away from him and points off somewhere, as if to tell Rob, "You're not helping, sir, so get on somewhere," and this makes you think, Good riddance. Both to you and Rob, you mean.

"Son," the cop says you, mic up, looking up, "you really don't havta do this, son." You wonder why he said "son" twice. "I can help you, son." Goddammit.

If. You. Don't. Shut. The. Hell. Up. "NO. YOU. CANNOT!" You yell this but it feels pointless. You pull "your" phone out.

11:26 A.M.

Words . . . Nothing but words come at you from behind, with blue suits on.

"Kid . . . take it easy."

You wince, then whorl your head around. . . .

You see coppers.

"Step back!" you say. "I'm warnin' ya!"

He's got both his hands in front of him, as if to say, "Okay, kid, take it easy . . . take it easy." He is taking two steps back. He and his partner. Don't get you started on his partner. The guy is all in the back of him, timid. He's new, probably. Most-likely.

Picture standing on a ledge, high, high up, and you can see a crowd looking at you from down below a building.

Picture two assiduous cops behind you who think they can talk you out of it.

Picture you hyperventilating! Now picture dying in some trite way.

"To die," you mutter under your breath, "is like living."

The cop with the hands that were up hears this. "What?" he says. "Dying is dying, kid. Take it easy. You don't wanna do this. Think of your mom or dad."

"I have no dad," you inform this asshole. "He's dead. And as for my mom, I barely speak to her. I barely speak to anyone."

"You don't have anyone?" the timid officer, the one standing behind the hand officer, chirps. Ha! "I'm sure you have somebody, sir."

Say sir one more time and I swear I'll gut you like a fish, you think. "No . . ." you start. "Um, no, nobody, sir."

"Hey. Listen. Let's talk, huh? What do ya—"

"Hold that thought," you say, interrupting the fag. You turn and look down at the crowd. "HEY, I WANNA—" You stop, squint, the turn back around. "Hey!" you say, noticing the cops a few steps more forward, looking like they were gonna pull you down or some shit. "Back up! You ain't trickin' me!" They stop and nod and then step back. You look back at the crowd. "SHELBY!" She's nowhere in sight. "SHELBY! SHEEELLLBBBYYY!"

The cop down below with the megaphone says, "She's trying to go up there."

"NO!" you blurt. "IF SHE DOES, I'LL JUMP, I SWEAR IT!"

The cop down below kind of freaks out. "Okay!" he says. "Take it easy." You see him press a button on the walkie-talkie on his shoulder. After a few moments of this, you see another cop point and direct. Shelby comes out. The megaphone cop says to you, "Okay, sir! She's back!"

"GOOD! SHELBY!"

She takes the megaphone from the cop. Takes a few seconds. "Yes, baby?" she says into it. "Why don't you want me up there?"

"BECAUSE!"

"Why?"

"BECAUSE I'M THIRSTY!"

"You're thirsty?!"

"YES!"

"Get this man a beer!"

Everyone down below kind of laughs.

"NO SERIOUSLY!" you shout. "I WANT A COKE!"

"We can arrange that, baby!" Shelby the Lovely says. "Is this, like, a last meal or something?"

You don't say anything.

"Right. Well, lets get this man a bee— I mean, a Coke." She lowers the megaphone.

But you "upper" "your" phone, though.

11:32 A.M.

Codswallop! All it is you're doing. You don't know a smatter of British slang, but hey, never too late to learn. It's never too late to learn anything. Such naiveté, such shit. So far, so good. You wait. "NOW!" you pretty much bewail. "I WANT COKE, NOW!!" You're like an infant. "PLEASE!" Now you're begging. "Alright, sir," one of the officers says behind you. "Take it easy. Real slow." Lop your F-ing head off! You maunder, "I iz no good more than I's go into dee room's toilet tree shower-filled killer body lover baby under bed to be under one of those literal kinds of Under The Sea Creatures that Disney once Tessa said to me once and this is bullshit . . ." and your brain hurts in lieu of the helpers around you granting a drinking wish. "What?" the cop says behind you. "You'll be okay, sir. We're gettin' you your Coke." Told ya. Don't mind the blarney. If cops were to catch you, it's off to the looney bin! "Stay back!" you command. You see Shelby down there putting her hair up in a bun. She looks like she's on a mission. She's passed the fearful part of the situation, it seems. "Scat!" she says with the megaphone. "Any guy up there better not touch my wittle ______!" And then she says, "Go up there, guys, and get him a Coke!" Up here where you're at, the officer mumbles, "Okay, bitch," thinking probably that you didn't hear him. And then snap goes a can. "Here you go, sir. Your Coke you requested." He steps forward to you. (You imagine him thinking you're a pussy.) "Stop!" you say. "Set it on top of the wall over there. Warnin' ya! I'll do it if you step closer!" "Oh," he says. "Okay." Then he walks on over, sets the can down, and walks back to his original spot like the lil' bitch his is right now, granting a suicidal's wish 'n' shit. Where did the Coke come from? you ask yourself. Oh well. Arms out. You walk on an invisible line and it's funny because if you were drunk then you wouldn't pass this "line" test, in theory, because that's what they give to drunk people. Down, down, down. There. You lean down and grab the Coke. It's snapped out, *duh!* You wish you were the one that could have done it. But oh well. People always do shit for you when you're crazy. You stand up, tilt your head back, and let the Coke just slide on down its metal, into your mouth, down your throat, down into your stomach, and burn the lining with acid. Making you fat. Chug. All gone. Crush. Throw metal. Litter. You feel a Shelby & you conversation coming. But before all that mess, you . . .

11:40 A.M.

"_____!" "YEAH?" "You know . . . you're selfish." "WHY?" "You have so much talent and so much going for you that it kind of makes me sick. People envy you!" "YEAH RIGHT! NO THEY DO NOT!" "They really do!" "ELABORATE!" "You treat people good, you're very nice, pleasant, and heck of a funny guy! You're not afraid, even though you think you are. I see that." "WELL I DON'T!" "You need to, _______. It could save a life!" "MY LIFE ISN'T WORTH SAVING!" "Talk to us, _______, we're all here! Tell us what's wrong! You want a voice, well, you got one! Go!" "SHELBY. BABY. I JUST WANT TO BE HAPPY AND I'M NOT! ALL THIS LIFE IS IS ABOUT MONEY, FAME, FORTUNE, TRYING TO MAKE IT BIG! I HATE HOW WE ALL LIVE—" "That's just Capitalism, sweetheart." "AT ANY RATE . . . It's NOT FAIR!" "Do you even try to work for it? Be honest." "NO!" "Well, baby, that's it! That's your problem! If you go for it then you'll see results. As some wise person once said, 'You'll lose one-hundred percent of your shots if you don't throw them up' or something like that." "BUT I WONDER IF THOSE SHOTS WILL EVEN BRING ME HAPPINESS!" "You won't know if you don't try, sweethe— Just get get down from that ledge, please! You're scaring me! This isn't the _______ that I know!" "YOU NEVER KNEW ME!" "Yes! I! Do!" "NO! YOU! DO! NOT! I JUST MET YOU YES-TERDAY!!" "And guess what . . ." "WHAT?" "You took the courage to show up at my house! *You* did that! You! Not anyone else! And now look, I'm totally in love with you!" "WHAT! YOU ARE?!" "YES!" "HOW?! I'M A MESS!" "But you're *my* mess. Look at the smile on my face! I love you, _______! I love love love you!!" "I LOVE YOU TOO!" "_______, I wanna show you some-thin'. See these people?" "YEAH . . . ?" "They see a troubled person that is so miserable that he wants to end his life. But they don't know you like I do. I don't see that guy. I see a man. I see a very strong, independent, happy man who just wants the best for the world. That's why I love you! You really do care!" "THESE

PEOPLE JUST SEE A LAME-ASS!!" "But you're not! And you should see that!" "I DON'T!" "Why?" "I KNOW THIS IS A SELFISH ACT WITH SELFISH CONSEQUENCES THAT CAN'T AND SHOULDN'T BE TAKEN LIGHTLY!" "I feel like you've said this before, hun! Just step down! Please!" "I WANNA DIE!" "Look. What if I just talk and you just listen, okay?" ". . ." "Okay. Happiness is not something that comes to you. People like to have fun and have material things, but that's not happiness. Those are just to make life interesting. The real happiness consist of freedom. Freedom comes from releasing all needs. You do have needs. You want to be loved and it's too much. You have to love yourself first. In order to have self-acceptance you gotta believe the possibility of happiness. It doesn't just come to you. Most people havta look at their lives from a different point and say, 'You know, it's not all bad to live right now. I have a great thing goin'. Sure. I'd like more, but hey, it's a journey. . . .' Did you know some people get depressed once they are unemployed, _____? Crazy. You'd think it'd be awesome to not work, but apparently humans need to have work so they can keep sane and find importance in life." "SUCH BULL." "It's okay, though, boobear." "I JUST WANT TO BE HAPPY, IS ALL I WANT!" "Look. You see this guy here, in the yellow shirt, this cop?" "YEAH . . . ?" "You don't know this but I know him. He's my cousin's friend. He's gay! That's why I flashed him earlier. We were playing along, see. Haha!" "Um, huh?" "Yeah!" "WHAT DOES HE HAVTA DO WITH THIS SHIT?" "I'm only sayin' that life isn't *all* bad! There's fun-ness in it, too! You gotta look passed all the bullshit drama." "It's HARD

TO. . . .” “_____, you know what. Just jump. Do it!” “Umm . . . I’M SORRY?” “Do it, pussy!” “I CAN’T BELIEVE YOU OF ALL PEOPLE WOULD EGG THIS ON!” “Babe, do it, if you think it’ll make you happy!” “IT WON’T!!” “Then get down from there!” “I’M TOO SCARED!” “Life is all about being scared, _____! You gotta face the music!” “I’M NOT PRE-PARED TO LIVE!” “You've lived your whole life! How’s about you get down and we go out to eat or something? Do you have any idea how much I care about you?” “BUT IT MAKES NO SENSE THAT YOU WOULD EGG ME ON, SHELBY!! WHY?!” “You don’t have the balls!” “HOW DO YOU KNOW THAT?! I COULD JUMP RIGHT NOW!!” “Then do it and STOP TALKING about it, pussy! Stop clenching your eyes and jump!” “I . . .” “JUMP!” “I can’t, um . . .” “JUMP, PUSSY!” “I can’t do it!” “_____, stop cryin’. It’s okay.” “NO It’s NOT!” “Why don’t you give yourself a second chance. The old _____ is behind you. This new _____ is the real you. Forget this sad _____; he’s a pussy. The new _____ has a girlfriend, a car, nice friends, nothing to worry about, and is very confident and always sure! Screw society, I agree! But we live in it, so who gives a shit! We are the ones that are number one! Come! Down! Here! No reason to die, _____! NO REASON! Just come down! We’ll—*I’ll* get you some help! Come down here and we’ll go home and make ice cream and have fun and tell stories and make love and kiss and be together and love for the first time and sign up for college and get better jobs and more money that we rightfully earn and can be proud of and we can sail the ocean and we can fish and party and nothing can stop us and we can pretend like the day doesn't end and we can be 'one' and we can smile and we can laugh and we can take one day at a time and be better people and we can continue to push forward. . . . And, above all else, we can live. . . . What d'ya say, huh? Come down! Give this living thing a chance. It's not easy and nobody is good at it, but it's what we got; it's *all* we got. So lets tackle it down together! Don't be all sad!" and these words of Shelby make you smile and then you turn around to lean down and slowly but surely scoot off the ledge and sit, dangling your feet facing away from the huge death drop, and the two cops, now at ease, come forward and help you down from the ledge and, bunk, you step down and wipe your pants off and turn around to see the sky isn't so bad, not like it used to be; it's bright and Florida-ey, and that's perfectly fine, perfectly A-O.K. This is what you want. Freeze frame. Look down.

11:52 A.M.

ain't shit but you have to fight through it. Plans change. The two cops, Mr. Lameboy and Mr. Punk-beezy, are at both your sides, sort of pushing you along, together, as you're walking toward the roof's elevator doors. Mr. Lameboy presses the button with his keys and then you think about how it's actually F-ed that you're totally making up names for these guys in your head.

They are only trying to help, do their jobs, and live a healthy, caring life.

The doors finally open and, oh look who it is, the elevator guy, the one with the funny-looking monkey hat who you saw yesterday and you totally told him to do his job and not mess with you, is standing there close to the panel, his head down, a smile on his face.

He looks up. The smile goes away. "Oh! Sorry, sirs!" he says, stepping even more aside than he already is.

Mr. Lameboy nods at him and Mr. Lameboy's partner and him tug you along into the elevator.

They two of them are at the back corners of the elevator, hands behind backs. You all four, the two cops, you, and the happyish elevator boy, are looking forward at the doors, possibly waiting for something, anything, to happen.

After a few long, freaking long moments of utter awkward silence, the elevator boy mumbles something to you.

"Hey man, you all right?"

"Yeah," you say. "Never been better."

"You gotta stay outta trouble, man—Or I mean sir." He clears his throat. "Eh-hem, sorry . . ."

"It's okay, man. You're all okay. Really."

"You're a lot nicer to me, sir," this elevator boy says to you, squinting, seemingly questioning your efforts of niceness. "You okay?"

You turn to him. "How did you not hear about the guy on the roof about to kill himself? Did you miss that whole spiel?"

He grins. "Nope."

You sigh, then say, "I guess I'm being nice so I can back out and be just another pussy. I was never gonna kill myself in the first place."

"Well, sir," the elevator boy says, pausing. "If, uh, you want to know my opinion on"—he faces you—"the situation, then ask me."

You laugh. "Okay. What do you think?"

"I think you just needed a reality check, is all. You're not a bad dude. I see you practically everyday before you go to work. I hear the conversations you have with people you briefly stand with. You're not a bad guy. I think you've changed, sir."

Your eyes light up! "Really?"

"Mhm. I do. You're not the same guy, though, from yesterday. Which is great, sir! You were a total . . . um—excuse my language—asstard."

You start laughing like a wild man, and the elevator boy does too; so do the cops, slightly.

"Thanks," you say to the elevator boy.

"Mhm. Don't mention it. My job is to give you good conversation."

You notice something. . . . "Say, dude," you say to the elevator boy, "what's that music playing?"

He laughs. "Calming, huh?"

"Yeah—it is."

"Most call it 'elevator music,' but I call it my—excuse my language again—'screw it' music."

"Hmm . . . Maybe that's what I need," you say.

"What do you need, sir?" the elevator boy asks, facing you.

"I needed my elevator music, my 'not give a crap' or 'exit,' like how you have. I need to let go and be free and say forget it."

"You should, sir! Glad I could—"

Bing! the elevator doors open. You're at the bottom floor, already. The doors go outward.

"We'll talk tomorrow," the elevator boy says to you.

The two cops get to both your sides and are starting to pull you along out the elevator doors. But before you leave the threshold with them, you tell the elevator boy, "Never thought tomorrow was tomorrow," though you think it makes no sense after saying it.

He nods, though, and that's all that matters. You all seem to know it makes sense. Happiness is on its way for you. The road to recovery is a long journey, _____, so you gotta push through the hard and always hope for another tomorrow. Whatever you do is "the now," like how Rob puts it. Nobody can take that away from you, not even—

"Baby!" a familiar, lovely, awesome voice says.

You turn your head around to face forward. You immediately grin.

It's Shelby. She's crying. Her tears are messing up her make-up. But you think it's sweet and the most beautiful thing ever. She's running toward you, saying, "My baby my baby my baby!"

You turn red, sort of. . . .

The cops let go of you because you're sure they think that she's way more important.

She hugs you, giving one of those tight ones, smothering you in love. "I love you," she says, then gives you a big, fat, wet kiss on your lips. Endorphins rush into your brain.

"Is this what happiness is?" you ask Shelby.

She nods. "Mhm. Yes, baby. It's called—"

Beep! beep! beep! "your" phone rings.

12:00 P.M.

It's called "living."

Photo: (c) Briana Fesh

kevin klix is a blogger, is an award-winning painter, and is a lover of photography. He lives in the city of Pittsburgh.

THE NOVELS OF **KEVIN KLIX**

BIFLOCKA
A Novel

ISBN 978-0-9965410-0-8 (paperback)

From his debut novel that catapolted Kevin Klix into the best-seller's list comes Clyde Clark, a highschool senior that comes in contact with a highly-toxic drug that is both lucrative and addicting to not only himself but his entire suburb of South Florida.

ELEVATOR MUSIC
A Novel

ISBN 978-0-9965410-4-6 (paperback)

"Great, powerful piece. . . . The real question: 'What is normal?' Venture and decide for yourself."
—Duy Lam, CEO of *Country Club Company*

A LION IN YOUR NUMBER
A Novel

ISBN 978-0-9965410-2-2 (paperback)

"Klix explores the question of Autism. With consistant voice, ambitious in scope, Klix has developed a novel that is easy, consuming, and poetic."
—Jonathan Spradlin, author of *American Creamy*

9 780099 654104 6